CONTENTS

Title Page
Copyright
Dedication
Epigraph
vATICAN HOLY SEE INVESTIGATIONS
THE MAIN CHARACTERS
THE SAVIOUR'S COMING
THE SAVIOUR'S COMING

THE MAIN CHARACTERS	1
THE MAIN CHARACTERS	3
AUTHOR'S THANKS	6
INSPIRATION	11
MY VERY REAL STORY CONTINUES TODAY	13
About The Author	17
Praise For Author	19
THE VATICAN MONSIGNOR	23
Books By This Author	25

THE VATICAN MONSIGNOR

THE SAVIOUR'S COMING

GERRY CULLEN

Copyright © 2024 GERRY CULLEN

All rights reserved

The characters and events portrayed in this book are fictitious. Any similarity to real persons, living or dead, is coincidental and not intended by the author.

No part of this book may be reproduced, or stored in a retrieval system, or transmitted in any form or by any means, electronic, mechanical, photocopying, recording, or otherwise, without express written permission of the publisher.

ISBN-13: 9798883728869
ISBN-10: 1477123456

Cover design by: Art Painter
Library of Congress Control Number: 2018675309
Printed in the United States of America

*THIS BOOK IS DEDICATED TO
MY MUM AND DAD*

VIA, VERITAS, VITA

I AM THE WAY ... THE TRUTH ... THE LIFE

THE VATICAN MONSIGNOR

Monsignor Kevin O'Flaherty is no ordinary priest. He loves the classics, has a taste for golf and Guinness, all things Irish, and a nose for solving the unknown.

The Monsignor is Head of Investigations at the Vatican. He reports directly to Cardinal Raphael and His Holiness, the Pope … Supreme Pontiff of Rome.

In this series of stories, The Monsignor, investigates into various mystical phenomena, around the World.

The Saviour's Coming is based on the Blessed Trinity … God in three persons, and it's the Monsignor's first investigation.

The Monsignor is assigned by Cardinal Raphael and the Holy Father. He teams up with Professor "Max" Brookstein in New York after being summoned by the Cardinal to investigate into recent, ongoing,

THY WILL BE DONE

NO SCIENTIFIC EXPLANATION
61

GUARDIANS OF THE
AFTERLIFE ... GUARDIANS
OF ALL IN THIS LIFE   76

THE ARC OF THE COVENANT
85

THE FINAL SOLUTION?
93

THE MAGDALENE MYSTERY

CRYPTIC MESSAGES
99

RENDEZVOUS
112

ENTRAPMENT
119

THE POWER AND THE GLORY

ECHOES OF THE PAST
125

A LINK TO THE CATACOMBS
138

A PERILOUS SITUATION
146

TIME FACTOR
152

SIGNS FROM HEAVEN

THE FIRST SIGN
156

NATION WILL RISE AGAINST NATION
166

THE END OF TIME?
173

BLESSED BE GOD, FOREVER
181

ONE SECOND FROM LIFE …
ONE SECOND FROM DEATH

TO KILL A PRESIDENT
187

HANGING BY A THREAD
198

UNSTOPPABLE
204

TIME SEQUENCE
211

DIAGRAMMA VERITAS (THE
DIAGRAM OF TRUTH)

GALILEO'S SECRET
218

ROMAN INTUITION
229

DIVINE EXPECTATIONS

THE MAIN CHARACTERS

Introducing ... Monsignor Kevin O'Flaherty.

The Monsignor is an unorthodox Irish Roman Catholic Priest, based at the Holy See in the Vatican, and Head of Investigations. He has a nose for solving the unknown.

The Monsignor is six feet tall, has brown hair and green eyes. He is in his mid forties, very astute, and is of a proud Irish background. He was ordained in Dublin, and possesses a sharp wit and sense of humour.A typical Irishman, with a lilting Dublin accent.

Favourite Quotes ... It's one thing to have knowledge but another thing to have wisdom. They see but they lack vision. How well can you know anyone?

The Monsignor has a keen interest in golf, all things Irish and loves the classics.

The Monsignor reports directly to Cardinal Raphael

and His Holiness the Pope, Supreme Pontiff of Rome.

Cardinal Raphael ... is a devout member of the College of Cardinals at the Palace of the Holy Office in the Vatican. He is astute and wise, a leader. He is a confidante of the Holy Father.

Cardinal Raphael ensures that the Monsignor is effective as Head of Investigations, and frequently sends him into unknown territory, on various assignments to find explanations.

Professor "Max" Brookstein is about five foot eight, slim build, has jet black long hair, blue eyes, in her mid thirties and attractive. She always dresses very smart in her designer suits and attire. You wouldn't think she was a Professor at all. She has a good sence of humour and has a flair for the extraordinary!

The Professor is based in New York city, and part of the Monsignor's Investigations unit. Both have a mutual respect for each other and work well together.

The Professor reports to Cardinal Raphael at the Vatican.

Professor Robert Kellerman is based in Oxford. He is renowned, and works with the Monsignor on various investigations. The Professor is an Oxford academic, he is five foot ten, has blue eyes, brown hair and has a professional look about him.

THE SAVIOUR'S COMING

This three part story introduces Monsignor Kevin O'Flaherty, a Roman Catholic priest, Head of Investigations at the Holy See in the Vatican.

This story is based on the Blessed Trinity – God in three persons.

God the Father ... God the Son, and God the Holy Ghost.

Monsignor Kevin O'Flaherty is dispatched from the Vatican by Cardinal Raphael and sent to New York to make contact with Professor "Max" Brookstein.

They have been given orders to check into recent phenomena to investigate if it is real or a hoax?

It's not too long before they find out the truth!

Earthquakes, tidal waves, famines and great signs in the Heavens follow. Evidence of The Second Coming signals the end of the World is at hand, or as we know it.

Nation rises against Nation, as predicted in the Book of Revelation, escalating possible nuclear war.

A time to act, to protect, and stop Russia attacking the United States, begins a final climax and countdown for the entire World.

Can Monsignor O'Flaherty and "Max" hatch a plan to save the World from impending doom and catastrophe?

Will they do it in time … and most importantly will God listen?

THE SAVIOUR'S COMING

THE BLESSED TRINITY ... GOD THE FATHER

God made us a family
We need one another
We love one another
We forgive one another
We work together
We worship together
Together we use God's word
Together we love all
Together we serve our God
Together we hope for Heaven
God is the supreme being and principal object of our faith.

God created Heaven and Earth in just seven days.

As the whole World awaits, The Second Coming ... God watches over us, and asks us to put all our trust in Him.

The Apocalypse is the complete and final destruction

of the World, and it is described in the Book of Revelation. An event involving total destruction on a catastrophic scale.

When signs are seen in the Heavens, the Vatican and the Holy See assign Monsignor Kevin O'Flaherty as Head of Investigations, and the battle of Armageddon begins the final war between human governments and God.

Is the end in sight?

The Monsignor has been summoned to meet Cardinal Raphael at the Palace of the Holy Office, in Vatican city.

The Monsignor is six feet tall, has brown hair and green eyes. He is in his mid forties, very astute, and is of a proud Irish background. He was ordained in Dublin, and possesses a sharp wit and sense of humour.

The Palace is an extra territorial property of Vatican city. It houses the Holy Office of the Roman Catholic Church. The Palace is situated near the Petrine Gate close to the Vatican. It has been converted into the seat of the Holy Office. The Palace was constructed in 1514 and is owned by the Holy See.

The Monsignor enters the palatial surroundings and is greeted by a Vatican aide.

He is asked to be seated in the main hall, awaiting arrival of Cardinal Raphael.

Several minutes later the Cardinal enters the meeting room.

"Good morning, Monsignor" greets the Cardinal

Monsignor O'Flaherty kneels and kisses the Cardinal's ring.

"Good morning, your excellency" replies O'Flaherty

"Are you aware of the recent phenomenon that is sweeping the World?" asks the Cardinal

"I am indeed, your excellency … in fact it is all over the news" advises the Monsignor

"We call it a phenomenon, as we need you to look into the truth" advises the Cardinal

"We?" asks the Monsignor

"I have discussed it at length, with the Holy Father" advises the Cardinal

"Great signs have been witnessed in the Heavens, Monsignor" explains the Cardinal

"What we need is for you to find out the truth … is it real or a hoax" advises the Cardinal

"That's where you come in" adds the Cardinal

"The Holy Father is God's Vicar on Earth" advises the Cardinal

"Where do we start, Eminence?" asks the Monsignor

"We have booked you on a flight to New York" advises the Cardinal

"New York?" asks the Monsignor

"You will be fully briefed, on your arrival" explains the Cardinal

"I will leave immediately, Eminence. I will look for answers and will advise you" replies the Monsignor

"Before you leave Monsignor, you will be teaming up with, Professor Max Brookstein, on your arrival, in New York" advises the Cardinal

The Monsignor kneels and kisses the Cardinal's ring …

"Good day, Monsignor" advises the Cardinal

"Good day, Eminence" replies the Monsignor

Monsignor O'Flaherty heads for Rome International Airport and links up with his scheduled flight to John F Kennedy International, New York.

Fiumicino – Leonardo da Vinci International Airport is situated several miles outside the Vatican.

The Monsignor enters Terminal 3 and checks in for his

flight to John F Kennedy International, New York.

"Boungiorno" greets the booking official

An attractive young woman in Gucci flight attire, addresses the Monsignor. She is typically very Italian.

"Do you require a window seat, Padre?" asks the young woman

"I don't mind" responds the Monsignor

"Your accent?" asks the young lady

"Oh, I'm Irish" replies the Monsignor

"Do you work at the Vatican?" asks the young lady

"How do you know, is it so obvious?" asks the Monsignor

"The Vatican coat of arms on your hand luggage" replies the young lady

"Yes, I do, how very astute of you" replies the Monsignor

"Your very distinguished" replies the young lady

"Thank you for the compliment … so are you" replies the Monsignor

The young woman laughs and blushes at the Monsignor's compliment.

The booking official hands back the flight tickets to the Monsignor.

"Have a pleasant flight, Padre" advises the official

"Thank you, I will" responds the Monsignor

The airport is a huge complex of terminals and other buildings.

It handles tens of millions of passengers every year, on their way to, and from the Italian city.

It is one of Europe's busiest airports with connections to a host of destinations across the World.

A voice on the internal electronic board system asks for all passengers to commence boarding …

"Passengers for Flight AV244, Rome International to John F Kennedy, New York please board at Gate 236" advises the announcer

"That's me" replies the Monsignor

All luggage has been carefully loaded onto the Italia Transporto Aero Airways flight.

The Monsignor is greeted at the plane entrance by wait

ing flight staff …

"Seat 7B on the left, Sir" advises a flight attendant

The plane quickly fills to capacity and starts to taxi along the runway.

Seated next to the Monsignor is a very nervous passenger.

Natalie is in her mid thirties, has long brown wavy hair, green eyes.

"I hate flying" advises the passenger

"How about you" asks the passenger

"Oh, par for the course" replies the Monsignor

"Your Irish, aren't you?" asks the lady passenger

"Yes, I am … call me Kevin" advises the Monsignor

"Well, it's a long way to John F Kennedy … call me Natalie" advises the young lady

"Business or pleasure?" asks Natalie

"Business I'm afraid" advises the Monsignor

"What type of business are you in?" asks Natalie

"This and that, you know" responds the Monsignor

"What about you … are you going for business or pleasure?" asks the Monsignor

"Both" replies Natalie

The Flight attendant starts to go through safety procedures on the aircraft, which lasts for several minutes.

"I still hate flying" advises Natalie

"The in flight entertainment might help" advises the Monsignor

"What do you think, Natalie?" asks the Monsignor

"Maybe Kevin, maybe" replies Natalie

"What did you say your line of work was" asks Natalie

"Quite persistent aren't you?" responds the Monsignor

"Very protective aren't you?" replies Natalie

"In my line of work, I have to be" replies the Monsignor

"Well, what line of work are you in?" asks Natalie

" I am actually a Roman Catholic Priest" answers the Monsignor

"Are you attached to the Vatican?" asks Natalie

"Well yes, as a matter of fact, I am" replies the Monsignor

"Are you high up in Vatican status?" asks Natalie

"No, I am just a humble Monsignor" replies the Monsignor

"Are you Irish?" asks Natalie

"Yes, I am, through and through" advises the Monsignor
"Now I understand" replies Natalie
An hour into the flight, the plane suddenly lunges 100 feet and seems to be out of control. It begins a frightening descent …

"Mayday … mayday" advises the captain
"This is John F Kennedy tower … what is your present location?" asks the voice

"We are over the Atlantic … several hours before we arrive in JFK" answers the captain
"Emergency procedures in place" advises the co-pilot

The warning lights in the cabin advise … seatbelts on!

The captain advises all the passengers to keep calm.
"There's no need to panic or to have any cause for alarm" advises the captain
"We are experiencing a lot of turbulence and we must correct our course" advises the captain

Turbulence is an irregular movement of air that can cause erratic changes in the altitude or angle of a plane. It feels like bumpiness, and it can be caused by atmospheric pressure, weather fronts or jet streams.

Natalie goes into melt down, due to the ongoing situation. The Monsignor tries to calm her down.
Suddenly a celestial vision in the Heavens appears …
"Look out of the window" shouts a passenger
The Eye of God appears in the clouds. It is actually the sun, that is surrounded by clouds, which makes it look like an impressive eye.

"What's happening?" asks a passenger
"It's a sign" advises the Monsignor

Monsignor O'Flaherty is not a lover of flight travel and takes out his mobile phone to record the footage as evidence of what's happening.

"Oh my God ... what must I do to be saved?" shouts another passenger

"Don't panic!" replies another passenger

"A disturbance in the Heavens ... is this the beginning of the last days?" asks another passenger

"What's happening?" asks Natalie

"You could say when these celestial signs happen, God has begun the final chapter of human history" advises the Monsignor

"What's going on?" asks another shocked passenger

"We may be drawing close to the end of time" responds the Monsignor

"We could be witnessing the end of the World" adds the Monsignor

"Your a Joab's comforter, aren't you?" advises a passenger

"Is the prophesy about to be fulfilled, Father?" shouts a passenger

"A little knowledge can be very dangerous" advises the Monsignor

"The one true God is here" replies another passenger

"Can you see it Father?" asks Natalie

"Yes, it's a sign from God" replies the Monsignor

Faces appear in the clouds and an incredible blinding light proclaims ...

"I am God ... the one and only ... open your eyes for the day is coming when the World will be no more ... be ready for you don't know the day or the hour" proclaims the voice in the clouds

"Did you get that, Father?" asks Natalie

"Yes, I think it's been recorded on my mobile phone" replies the Monsignor

As Monsignor O'Flaherty replays the footage, with amazing sound, the captain announces that the airliner is back in control, and about to land at John F Kennedy International, New York.

John F. Kennedy is the main International airport serving New York. It handles tens of millions of passengers every year. It has recently been redesigned to handle more passengers for the future.

The airport announcer advises the arrival of Flight AV244 from Rome International …

"Passengers now arriving on Flight AV244 Rome to John F Kennedy International … Gate 275" advises the announcer

Natalie bids the Monsignor farewell in the arrivals lounge.

"It was nice to chit chat with you" advises the Monsignor

"Chit chat?" asks Natalie

"I get the feeling that no one says chit chat these days?" asks the Monsignor

Natalie begins to laugh.

"Well, your right, no one really does, Father" replies Natalie

"Wonderful to meet you anyway … have a nice time in New York" responds the Monsignor

"Have a nice day, maybe we'll bump into each other again?" advises Natalie

The Monsignor continues to move across the walkways into the Arrivals Terminal ...

Waiting to meet the Monsignor at the gate with lots of other people is Professor "Max" Brookstein who is on secondment to the Vatican.

The Monsignor looks around the waiting arrivals lounge but sees no one waiting to greet him, then suddenly he hears a voice.

"Monsignor O'Flaherty?" asks the voice

"Yes, I'm Monsignor O'Flaherty" replies the Monsignor

"Hi I'm Max ... lovely to meet you" replies the voice

"A woman" responds the Monsignor

"How very perceptive of you, Monsignor" replies the voice

"Yes Father, I am ... I hope I've not disappointed you?" replies the voice

"No, sorry ... I was expecting ... " replies the Monsignor cautiously

"Well, I don't know what I was expecting, to be sure" advises the Monsignor

"Well, hello ... I'm actually called Maxine ... but you can call me Max" advises the Professor

Professor "Max" Brookstein is about five foot eight, slim build, has long jet black hair, blue eyes, in her mid thirties and attractive. She looks very smart in her navy suit and white blouse. You wouldn't think she was a Professor at all.

The Monsignor is carrying a Papal briefcase.

"Well, you couldn't have made it more obvious than it is" adds Max

xxx

"Obvious in what way, Max?" asks the Monsignor
"Your not exactly wearing a disguise are you?" advises Max
"The Papal coat of arms on your briefcase for instance" replies Max
"Well no lass, not exactly" replies the Monsignor
"Did Cardinal Raphael send you?" asks Max
"Yes, I'm head of Investigations for the Holy See" advises the Monsignor
"I've been asked to make contact with you by Cardinal Raphael" explains the Monsignor
"and I suppose he never mentioned that you'd be working with a woman" asks Max
"Well to be precise, no, he didn't" advises the Monsignor
"Did you have a pleasant journey?" asks Max
"It was eventful to say the least, but I've managed to capture some of it on my mobile phone" advises the Monsignor
"So English … mobile phone" advises Max
"Actually, I'm Irish" advises the Monsignor
Max apologises for her misunderstanding.
Max invites the Monsignor to have a cup of coffee at a nearby coffee shop in the Airport.
"OK I agree, but only if you'll allow me to pay" advises the Monsignor
"It's a deal, Monsignor" advises Max
"Oh, please call me Kevin … that's way too formal" advises the Monsignor
"Thank you Kevin, I will" replies Max
The Monsignor orders two coffees with cakes to

be brought to their table, and the conversation continues ...
"Well, what did you record on your phone?" asks Max
The Monsignor plays the captured footage to Max.
"What is it?" asks Max
"It could be a sign of the end of the World" replies the Monsignor
"The so called Eye of God" advises the Monsignor
"The apocalypse?" asks Max
"It could be ... maybe a prewarning of what's to come" advises the Monsignor
"What's to come?" asks Max
Max views the footage on the Monsignor's phone.
"And so it begins" advises Max
"What exactly are you a Professor of?" asks the Monsignor
"Oh, I'm a Professor of Science and Religion ... I also specialise in strange phenomena" advises Max
"Is that what this is ... a strange phenomenon?" asks the Monsignor
"Surely that's what we have to find out" replies Max
"All I know is that it is, one thing to have knowledge and another thing to have wisdom" advises the Monsignor
"Wisdom?" asks Max
"Figuratively speaking of course" replies the Monsignor
"Cardinal Raphael has asked us to find proof, beyond all reasonable doubt" advises Max
"Take another look at the footage, and listen to the voice" advises the Monsignor

Max reviews the footage and listens to the voice on the recording for a second time.
"It doesn't sound like a hoax to me" advises the Monsignor
"I'm convinced too, Kevin" responds Max
"We'll need all the help we can to get through this" advises Max
"Yes, and God's help too" replies the Monsignor
Max and the Monsignor leave the coffee shop and the airport terminal.
Outside, on the airport concourse, someone is wearing a sandwich board proclaiming ... The end of the World is nigh! They start shouting for the World to be changed now!
"They lack inner vision" advises the Monsignor
"But do you know what, they are probably right" adds the Monsignor
Max's cell phone starts to ring ...
"OK, we're on our way" advises Max
"What's happening Max?" asks the Monsignor
"Another sign in the sky has been seen ... we need to head down town to see it" advises Max
Both Max and the Monsignor hot foot it to the waiting taxis. The driver loads up the Monsignor's suitcases into the car boot.
"Where to, Mac?" asks the driver
"Central park" advises Max
"Step on it" asks the Monsignor
The taxi negotiates the busy traffic and arrives at Central Park, in a matter of minutes.
Max pays the taxi driver. The Monsignor and Max

proceed on foot into Central Park.
"Have a nice day" advises the driver
"You too" replies the Monsignor
Another phenomenon is now visual, for all to see.
A blood red moon can be seen clearly in an almost cloudless sky.
The Monsignor suddenly remembers a verse in the Bible written by Matthew.
"When evening comes, you will say it will be fair weather, for the sky is red and in the morning, it will be stormy for the sky is red and overcast. You can read the appearance of the sky, why can't you read the sign of the times?" quotes the Monsignor
"What does it mean, Kevin?" asks Max
"This is a sign of the times ... the shape of things to come, Max" advises the Monsignor
"A sign of what?" asks Max
"It's a prophetic sign ... a warning or prewarning of what's to come" continues the Monsignor
"What's to come?" replies Max
"The predicted end of time ... the apocalypse ... this could really be the end" responds the Monsignor
"We must inform Cardinal Raphael and the Vatican of our findings" advises Max
"This is no hoax" replies the Monsignor
"It really is a sign for all mankind, that time is running out" advises the Monsignor
"And what about the governments?" asks Max
"All their powers will be rendered useless ... it could be the end of times" replies the Monsignor
"The ten signs of tribulation are near" advises the

Monsignor

"What are they?" asks Max

"Decapitation, dissension, devastation, disease, disasters, death, disloyalty, delusion, defection and declaration" advises the Monsignor

"It could be the end of the World" advises the Monsignor

The blood red moon continues to draw near to the Earth.

"All we can do is be ready and prepare" explains the Monsignor

"How do we prepare for such a massive awakening?" asks Max

"Shouldn't we warn the President?" asks Max

"Yes, but I've got a feeling he will already be on to this" advises the Monsignor

"God is the key … it may take an eternity … the sky foretells the end of the World" advises the Monsignor

"It's frightening" advises Max

"We must act quickly, and advise the United States government" advises Max

Suddenly, the ground and buildings start to shake …

"Earthquake" warns an official. People are terrified of the sudden movement.

"Take cover" shouts a passing police officer

Max and the Monsignor run for cover and just make it in time.

"An earthquake in down town New York?" asks Max

The earthquake lasts for several minutes.

Max and the Monsignor manage to reach safety at a hotel in Manhattan.

The story about the quake is all over the news.
A TV production company has managed to capture the whole unfolding situation, which is being played over and over on the 24 hour News bulletins ...
"That was a big one" advises a Newscaster
"7.5 on the Richter scale ... there's already been many reports of buildings collapsing in the centre of New York" adds the reporter
"This is no drill" warns the reporter
Blasting out on the radio are warnings to take cover and shelter in the subways with songs proclaiming the second coming is at hand.
"That really was a quake of some magnitude and force" advises Max
"What next?" asks the Monsignor
The News centre proclaims there is damage all over the city, and that a tidal wave may be imminent after the quake.
"If that happens it could wipe out New York city" warns Max
The National Guard are put on standby awaiting the President's orders.
"There is no escape ... no where to go" advises Max
"We can only hope, and pray that never happens" responds the Monsignor
The news soon reaches the Vatican. Cardinal Raphael and the Holy Father are in talks about the magnitude of the unfolding situation.
"What can we do Holy Father?" asks the Cardinal
"We have no forces against the power of God" advises the Pontiff

"We have faith and belief, and that is all that God wants" explains the Pontiff

"We cannot stop the apocalypse from happening … it was foretold long ago" advises the Pontiff

"Are we defenceless?" asks Cardinal Raphael

"We are all in God's hands" replies the Pontiff

Meanwhile, back in New York, the Monsignor and Max are investigating into the prophecies and cosmic signs concerning the announcement of Jesus's Second Coming.

News channels are contemplating what will happen in the coming days.

"Is it the end of the World as we know it?" asks a newscaster

"Are we about the witness the Second Coming?" adds the newscaster

"The prophetic sign will be visible to the entire World, and it will proclaim that the end of the World is imminent" advises the Monsignor

The sign of the end of age is a sign of hope for Jesus's disciples to let them know that the Rapture is at hand. The stars will fall to the Earth … the sky will be no more and every mountain and island will be removed. The Heavenly bodies will be shaken.

For all who are left on Earth there will be a time of famine.

A prophetic sign … God will reveal Himself to the World.

"There will be wonders in the Heavens" advises the Monsignor

"We are about to witness the end, and the beginning

of a new time" advises the Monsignor
"A new time?" asks Max
"Our Hearts will be opened and God will seal our fate" explains the Monsignor

THE BLESSED TRINITY
– GOD THE SON

The prophecy speaks of a child …
A Messiah from the lowest of men to the highest of Kings.
A star will come forth.
How long will it be?
It will not be years.

Hail … Hail
"Do not be afraid Mary for you have found favour with God" advises the Angel
"You will conceive, and give birth to a son … and
you will call him JESUS … the saviour" explains the Angel

"The Holy Spirit will come upon you and the power from the most High will overshadow you" … advises the Angel
"The Holy offspring will be called … The Son of God"

explains the Angel

"For nothing set by God can be impossible" advises the Angel

"Let it be done to me according to your word" replies Mary

"The Messiah will save us"
"He will come to deliver us"
"To deliver our people … Israel"
"Hail, Son of David"

"That is what the readings teach us" advises the Monsignor

"God the Son … proclaimed by the Angel of the Lord" explains the Monsignor

"And what of the prophecy?" asks Max

"They took it to be a myth, yet it was unwise of them to think of the prophecy too lightly" advises the Monsignor

"The three stars came to touch for the first time in 3,000 years" explains the Monsignor

"And what of Mary?" asks Max

The Monsignor continues to quote from the Bible.

"Do not be afraid to take Mary as your wife, Joseph" advises the Monsignor

"For she has been filled with the Holy Spirit, and He will bear the name of Jesus … the Saviour" advises the Monsignor

"The Son of God?" asks Max

"Truly, the Son of God" replies the Monsignor

"Yes, the very same, who was led to Calvary and

crucified for all the World to see" explains the Monsignor

"And what of today?" asks Max

"He lives today ... now and forever" replies the Monsignor

"The Light of the Lord will open the eyes of all who see" advises the Monsignor

"And those who don't?" asks Max

The Monsignor is cautious in his reply.

"God will open the eyes of everyone" replies the Monsignor

"A child will be ruler of all?" asks Max

"A miracle ... sent by God to save the World" responds the Monsignor

"God made man ... flesh of my flesh" advises the Monsignor

"The King of Kings" quotes the Monsignor

"How is your faith now?" asks the Monsignor

"Very moved and inspired, Kevin" answers Max

The Monsignor reads the quotes from his Bible.

"Rejoice, I bring you tidings of great joy" advises the Monsignor

"Who?" asks Max

"I am quoting the words spoken by the Archangel Gabriel" replies the Monsignor

"What else did he say?" asks Max

The Monsignor continues to quote from his Bible.

"For unto you, born this day, a Saviour, in the city of David ... who is Christ the Lord ... The Saviour" advises the Monsignor

"And now, The Messiah is set to return?" asks Max

"Yes, and I have my strength in God" replies the Monsignor

"He is for all mankind … for the whole World" advises the Monsignor

"Don't you mean … all humankind?" asks Max

"Yes, of course, we all must be politically correct these days, for all humankind" replies the Monsignor

"We are each given a gift" adds the Monsignor

A waiter attends their table in the swish hotel. They are carrying on as if nothing has happened.

The Monsignor asks the waiter a question.

"Has there been any more news concerning the recent earthquake?" asks the Monsignor

The waiter responds, and advises the Monsignor that the situation in down town New York is becoming more and more untenable.

"Why are you all so calm?" asks the Monsignor

"Unless we are told otherwise, it's business as usual" advises the waiter

"Max" orders a pot of coffee and refreshments.

The TV news channels are reporting 24 hours a day, and their continuing coverage of the recent earthquake, and pending tidal wave reaches a critical stage.

"We interrupt this broadcast to bring you the very latest on the situation, in New York City" advises the Newscaster

"The President has sent in the National Guard. We will update you on all developments every 30 minutes. Keep this channel open, and await further instructions" continues the Newscaster

Suddenly, several men in dark suits arrive at the Monsignor's table.
They flash their identification cards and ask for co-operation.
"FBI" advises one of the men
"Are you Professor Brookstein" asks one of the men
"Yes, I'm Professor Brookstein" replies Max
"Then you must be Monsignor Kevin O'Flaherty?" asks another man
"Yes, I'm O'Flaherty … how can we help you?" asks the Monsignor
"We've been instructed, to lead you to a place of safety" advises one of the men
"We're not going anywhere, until you tell us why" adds the Monsignor
A burly man enters and takes charge of the situation.
"My name is Jack Davenport. I'm a senior Special Agent with the FBI. We are under Presidential orders to take you to a secret location" advises Davenport
"Presidential orders?" asks Max
"The situation is becoming untenable" advises Davenport
"Well, are you going to come with us?" asks Davenport
"OK, we'll do as you say … on one condition" advises Max
"What condition?" replies Davenport
"That we speak directly to the President in person" continues Max
"I'm afraid, that is out of the question" replies Davenport
"Well, that's the condition lad, take it or leave it"

advises the Monsignor

"You know, we could have you deported in an instant" advises Davenport

"You can't deport me" advises Max

"I am an American national" explains Max

"And I am on a diplomatic investigation and acting within International Law" advises the Monsignor

The FBI agents whisper to each other, and decide to agree to the demands.

"OK, we'll see what we can do" advises Davenport

"And the President?" asks Max

"We'll keep you updated on that matter too" replies Davenport

"Now will you please follow us? Transportation has been arranged and awaiting your embarkation" advises Davenport

"Where are you taking us?" asks the Monsignor

"I've just told you … to a place of safety" advises Davenport

"We're not allowed to advise where" explains Davenport

"OK, we agree" advises Max

The Monsignor and Max are basically frog marched out of the hotel to a waiting blacked out limo and escorted into it by armed FBI agents. The black limo is flanked by Presidential vehicles front and rear.

After a 20 minute journey they arrive at a secret underground location, somewhere in New York city.

Max and the Monsignor are taken to a waiting area, somewhere in a large building. FBI agents are placed at the entrance. The location is very secure.

Suddenly, the doors open, and in walks several secret service agents. They are guarding a tall man in the middle.

It turns out to be the President of the United States, Jefferson Parker.

The Monsignor and Max are shocked to see who it is ...

"Good afternoon, you asked to see me?" asks the President

"Well" answers the Monsignor

"Thank you for seeing us, Mr President" replies Max

"We have a very grave situation on our hands. I have been fully briefed and I am aware of your investigation" advises the President

"The Holy Office at the Vatican have been in touch, and obviously we have sanctioned the authority for you both to work together on American soil" explains the President

"Where are you taking us?" asks the Monsignor

"You and I are being taken to another secure location" advises the President

FBI agents escort the Monsignor, Max, and the President to another room in the secret location.

All are seated at an extra long table, and the meeting begins.

"So, I have agreed to your request to see me, now how can I help you?" asks the President

The Monsignor begins to put forward the information he has received and updates the President.

"The day and the hour has been set and chosen" advises the Monsignor

"Who has done this?" asks the President

"The almighty … God" replies the Monsignor
"Are you a believer, Mr President?" asks Max
"Yes, naturally, I am" replies the President
"Please continue Monsignor" asks the President
"He who has risen from the dead is coming back to deliver all of us" advises the Monsignor
"In what way?" asks the President
"We believe that God, is in three persons … the Blessed Trinity" advises the Monsignor
"How can this be?" asks Max
"God The Father … God The Son and God The Holy Ghost" answers the Monsignor
"What does it all mean?" asks the President
"It means, Mr President, that the power of God is magnificent, a super nova, and there is no power on Earth that can stop it" advises the Monsignor
"It's our very being, our very existence … it's why we're here" explains the Monsignor
"Do you think God will destroy the Earth?" asks the President
"No, it will serve no purpose … but it could be the dawn of a new time" advises the Monsignor
FBI agents enter the room, and turn on the bank of televisions.
NEWSFLASH …
"The Rapture is taking place" advises a Newscaster
"It has begun" advises the Monsignor
Suddenly, George Winters, Chief of staff to the President, enters the meeting.
"Come in George" advises the President
"Sorry to barge in Mr. President, but there have been

developments concerning changes in atmospheric conditions throughout the country" advises Winters

"What's happening?" asks the President

"Reports of devastating 500 mph hurricanes across America" advises Winters

"Where and when did this happen?" asks the President

"It's not clear what this storm is or where it began" advises Winters

"My God" advises the President

"Why is this happening?" asks Max

"Why is God allowing this to happen?" asks the President

A News report is taking place on television across all 24 hour channels.

"Turn up the volume so we can hear what they have to say" asks the President

The multi channel televisions are now all showing the same broadcast.

"It's the beginning of the seven year period of tribulation" advises a newscaster

"What does that mean?" asks the President

"It means all believers will be saved into Heaven … but then the Antichrist will appear" advises the Monsignor

"The Antichrist?" asks Max

"Satan" replies the Monsignor

The Chief of Staff continues to update and brief the President.

"A 1,000 square mile zone is now in place" advises Winters

"How long do we have?" asks the President
"We only have minutes before it hits land" advises Winters
"All communications including satellite links are down" explains Winters
"The National Guard have been called up Mr President" advises Winters
The Newscaster continues to update the public on the current situation.
"These are signs of the Second Coming" advises the Monsignor
"It may seem overwhelming … but it's not the end" explains the Monsignor
"Yes … the Biblical prophecy" replies Max
"I remember" advises the President
"It speaks of wars, and rumours of wars … such things will happen" advises the Monsignor
The Monsignor produces a Bible from his Papal briefcase …
"I must go on television and address the nation" advises the President
"Is this how it should be?" asks Max
"Why are we being punished?" adds Max
"How can we stop it?" asks the President
"You can't" replies the Monsignor
"Only God can stop it" explains the Monsignor
Meanwhile, devastation is taking place across the World.
"There may be a way of stopping it, Mr President" advises the Chief of Staff
"How?" asks the President

Scientific Advisers enter the room, and update the President on their findings.

"We have calculations to stop the storm" advises a Scientist

"And you are" asks the President

"Doctor Stuart Peterson" advises the Scientist

"OK, Doctor lets hear your plan" asks the President

The Scientist briefs the President and the Chief of staff.

"Can it be done?" asks the President

"Do we have satellite capability?" asks the President

"We are working on it Mr President" advises Winters

Torrential rain with thunder and lightening continue to move inland. Oceans begin to rise. Across the World many other countries are also in it's grip.

All radio transmissions are now rendered inoperable.

"Get me on the News channels fast … this will be a blanket announcement" advises the President

"How long do we have?" asks the President

"Not long enough" advises the Chief of staff

BREAKING NEWS FLASH …

"An airliner is plunging to Earth" advises a Newscaster

"My God" responds the President

"Reports are coming in confirming this" adds the Newscaster

Winters updates the President concerning the satellites.

"We have been advised that communication systems are all back on line! Our satellites are tracking something of great magnitude" advises Winters

"What's happening?" asks the President

"We'll keep you posted Mr President" advises Winters

The President has now been taken to another room, in the secret complex, and has been wired up for an address to the nation.

All television channels are carrying the communication.

"Stand by for a message from the President" advises a reporter

The President is counted in by a television producer and begins to put forward his speech to the entire American nation. It is broadcast in all fifty states.

"My fellow Americans … the World is in turmoil. We are in the grip of something which is more serious than we have ever encountered, and it affects all human life on Earth" advises the President

The President continues his address to the nation.

"We have all seen the signs in the Heavens … some will say unexplained, but I fully believe that we're in the days of the Rapture, as indicated in the Bible … the end may not be far away. There may be terrible times ahead, yet you and I, my fellow Americans, will prevail. To all those who don't believe I will say that God is about to finally deliver His verdict on all our lives and that no one will be exempt from The Second Coming" advises the President

"God Bless You all" concludes the President

Meanwhile, in Vatican city, the Pope gives his papal address from the balcony of Saint Peter's to the thousands gathered in Vatican square.

"To all God's children, and peoples of the World. We may well be in the last days of the World as we know it ... great signs have been seen in the Heavens, yet there is more to come. There will be even more signs in the sun, moon and the stars. Our nations are in anguish and our seas are ferocious" advises the Pope

"The Lord will come like a thief in the night. Be ready, for we don't know when that day will come. The Gospel of the Kingdom will be preached to the whole World as a testimony to all nations, and then the end will come. So, I say again, be prepared for we don't know when that day will come. Be ready for the coming of The Lord and his unannounced return. When all these things happen look to the Heavens, for your redemption draws near" advises the Pontiff

Back in New York, the Monsignor and Max have now left the Presidential bunker and have been returned to their hotel by FBI secret service agents.

A message on the Monsignor's mobile phone instructs both of them to go to Saint John the Baptist Church in Manhattan.

"We've been instructed to go to a church in Manhattan" advises the Monsignor

"Where, exactly?" asks Max

The Monsignor advises the coordinates and both leave the hotel and jump into Max's waiting SUV.

"We may encounter problems along the way" advises Max

"Give me the address and I will programme it into the satellite navigation system" replies Max

"Navigation?" asks the Monsignor

"Yes, we will be guided by satellite to our destination" replies Max

The Monsignor advises Max the exact location.

"OK, it's on 211 (Two Eleven) West 30th Street and in the neighbourhood of Manhattan" advises the Monsignor

"OK, Kevin, the fastest route has now been programmed" advises Max

"Amazing" replies the Monsignor

"Can we step on it Max" asks the Monsignor

"OK, hold on to your hat" advises Max

"I'm not wearing one, lass" replies the Monsignor

"Just a figure of speech, Kevin" responds Max

"I knew that, I just wanted to hear your explanation" laughs the Monsignor

Saint John the Baptist is an old traditional church of some magnificence.

After negotiating all the traffic in New York they eventually arrive outside of the church of Saint John the Baptist.

Max and the Monsignor are met by two nuns, Sister Augustine and Sister Mary.

"Welcome, Monsignor" advises Sister Augustine

"Thank you" replies the Monsignor

"This is Max, sorry Professor Max Brookstein" advises the Monsignor

"Are you Jewish?" asks Sister Mary

"Yes, as a matter of fact, I am" replies Max

"We are all one, under the circumstances" advises the Monsignor

"God loves us all sister" responds the Monsignor
Another character arrives on the scene.
"Hi, I'm Father McGovern" says a voice
"Wonderful to meet you, your Eminence" replies Father McGovern
"OK, you can cut out the formalities Father" advises the Monsignor
"The World is in turmoil, there is no escape" advises Father McGovern
"We're hoping to find a way out" advises Max
"Why are you here?" asks Sister Augustine
"We have both been seconded by the Vatican, and the American government" advises the Monsignor
Suddenly, a parishioner asks a question.
"Tell me Father, how can I obtain eternal life?" asks the parishioner
"Just be who you are … let God do the rest" replies the Monsignor
Lots of beggars, and non believers are congregating outside of the church.
Father McGovern leads the Monsignor and Max into the inside of the building.
Saint John the Baptist is a very old traditional Roman Catholic church.
"It's a wonderful setting" advises the Monsignor
"Truly amazing" advises Max
"We specialise in spiritual, social and personal development, and welfare of all our parishioners" advises Father McGovern
"It truly is magnificent" responds the Monsignor
Father McGovern takes Max and the Monsignor into

the presbytery.

"Have you seen the news?" asks the House Keeper

Father McGovern turns on the television.

The News teams on all channels are continually updating everyone in New York city of the pending situation.

"Another earthquake is due to hit with smaller quakes all over the city" advises the newscaster

"This could be the big one" explains the newscaster

"The one to end everything?" asks the Monsignor

"Is there anything we can do?" asks Father McGovern

"Pray Father, that's all we can do" advises the Monsignor

"Our fate is sealed, and in God's hands now" replies the priest

"There is one thing you could do" advises the Monsignor

"Let everyone into the church … let it be a sanctuary for all" explains the Monsignor

"God will protect those in His care … for this is hallowed ground" advises the Monsignor

"Hallowed ground?" asks Max

"Yes, Max" replies the Monsignor

"God will not touch anyone on hallowed ground" advises the Monsignor

Sister Augustine, and Sister Mary now enter the presbytery.

"The Second Coming is here! Jesus said I will come again and receive you unto myself so that where I am you may be also" advises Sister Mary

Evacuation continues on a grand scale in New York

city. Everyone has been instructed to take to higher ground. The Freeways are jammed with traffic, and there is no movement in or out of John F. Kennedy International.

Back in Washington, the President, is addressing his Chief of Staff about the impending situation.

"How long do we have, George?" asks the President

"Not long enough, I'm afraid" replies the Chief of Staff

"Storm shelters ... we must get the people to safety" advises the President.

"We must focus on survival" adds the President

"There must be something we can do" replies the Chief of Staff

Tornados and hurricanes are causing massive destruction in the south, and are heading inland.

The President contacts Professor Brookstein on her cell phone.

Max's cell phone begins to ring.

"Mr President" replies Max

"Put the call on speaker Professor, I want the Monsignor to hear this too" advises the President

Max puts the call on speaker as instructed.

"OK, on behalf of the US government do what you can" advises the President

Max and the Monsignor vow to do everything in their power to help.

Someone in the background updates the President of the current situation.

"Mr President it's time to go" advises the Chief of Staff

The President is hurried away by armed Secret Service Agents

The call from the President is dramatically cut short.
Max and the Monsignor decide there may be something they could put in place to help the situation.
"Is it really the end of everything we've ever known" asks Father McGovern
"What's the current situation news wise?" asks the Monsignor
"The government has asked for full evacuation for all low ground cities, and to take to higher ground" advises Sister Mary
"We're in deep trouble" advises the Monsignor
"Can you see a way out of this?" asks Max
"How do you stop something like this?" replies the Monsignor
The Monsignor is deep in thought, and after a period of thinking suddenly advises there may be a way out.
"There could be a way, Max" advises the Monsignor
"What have you got in mind, Kevin?" asks Max
"God so much loved the Earth that He sent His only Son that He might save it" advises the Monsignor
"What does this mean for all the people of the World?" asks Max
"Don't you see?" replies the Monsignor
"See what?" asks Max
"We may be able to save the earth" advises the Monsignor
"Sorry, I don't follow … how can we save it, we are mere mortals?" asks Max
The News channels advise of a further impending disaster.

BREAKING NEWS …
"A further earthquake is expected to hit down town New York city in the next few hours. Predictions say it could hit 10.5 on the Richter scale. It will have extraordinary power, and cause catastrophic destruction, brace yourselves" advises the newscaster
"This will be followed by a tidal wave of dynamic proportions … move to higher ground as soon as you can" continues the newscaster
"If you can" replies the Monsignor
"How much time do we have?" asks Father McGovern
"Don't talk of time, man" advises the Monsignor
Back at the Vatican, the Pope is in communication, and in a meeting with all the Cardinals.
The Pontiff asks Cardinal Raphael for an update concerning Monsignor O'Flaherty.
"Cardinal Raphael has Monsignor O'Flaherty made contact with Professor Brookstein?" asks the Holy Father
"Yes, your Holiness" advises the Cardinal
"He has also been in contact with the President of the United States, and both have put forward their opinions on the matter" continues the Cardinal
"Are we about to witness catastrophic events all over the World?" asks the Pontiff
"We must turn to the Bible, Holy Father for answers" advises Cardinal Raphael
The Cardinal continues to update the Pontiff and all the other Cardinals.
"It says in Revelation … Behold, He is coming within the clouds and every eye shall see Him. It will be like

brightness of lightening illuminating the entire sky from east to west" advises the Cardinal

"What else does it say?" asks the Pontiff

"That Jesus is coming with power, and great glory, and with the sound of great trumpets that will awaken all who righteously are dead, and all will be gathered from the ends of the earth" informs the Cardinal

"All?" asks the Holy Father

"Yes, your Holiness ... all" replies the Cardinal

" ... but there is also a warning" advises Cardinal Raphael

Meanwhile across Europe and the far East, all major cities are experiencing damaging earthquakes and floods. In Egypt swarms of locusts on a Biblical scale are heading towards Cairo.

In Russia the situation worsens when the Military Generals inform their President that they must arm all nuclear weapons to stave off any threat from the West.

Moscow warns it may be forced to use nuclear weapons if a counter offensive is launched.

At the Kremlin, the Russian President is being brought up to speed by his Military Command.

Russian President Egor Novikov is a middle aged man, of slight build, has brown hair and a rugged complexion. He is a stickler for being shrewd.

"So, General Petrov, how are placed strategically?" asks the Russian President

"We have deployed half of our nuclear arsenal to Belarus" advises Petrov

"And the threat from the Americans and NATO?" asks

Novikov
"We will meet any counter attack. We are prepared for nuclear war" advises Petrov
"All we need is your instructions to launch the attack" advises Petrov
Back in Washington, the President, Jefferson Parker is also being brought up to speed concerning the threat of nuclear war.
Chief of Staff, George Winters, and several other Generals are in talks with the President in the Oval Office at the White House in Washington.
"Our Military command advise Russia is preparing for a nuclear attack, and has deployed half it's nuclear capability to Belarus" advises General Winters
"Why Belarus?" asks the President
"It's nuclear strike can be devastating from there" advises Winters
"Put all our nuclear arsenal on standby" advises the President
"We must be ready for any eventuality" explains the President
Back in Rome, Cardinal Raphael continues to update the Pontiff, and all the other Cardinals.
"The warning your Holiness … is to be ready, as the day may come unexpectedly … we all must watch and pray that we may be counted to stand worthy to escape all these things … for they will come to pass, and to stand before the Son of Man" advises the Cardinal
Back in down town New York, Max and the Monsignor venture out of the church of Saint John the Baptist and

find many lost souls on the road to nowhere.

The Monsignor is met with questions from every angle.

"Tell me priest, how are we to live now?" asks a stranger

"I care not for you or your God" says another

The Monsignor is cautious before he gives his reply.

"Get behind me Satan … it is the Antichrist that speaks" replies the Monsignor

The Monsignor continues to be cautious.

"Leave this man, I command you" advises the Monsignor

And with those words the man returns to his normal self.

"What happened?" asks the stranger

"My God, how did that happen?" asks the Monsignor

"Your righteous in the eyes of God" replies Max

"That's how Father" responds Max

"Praise be to God … and Bless His Holy name" replies the Monsignor

Max and the Monsignor continue walking and find a group proclaiming the Good News at a street corner.

"The coming of the Lord will not come to save those who are wicked, only to save those who are righteous, and truly believe in the word of God" advises a Preacher

"For God sees everything. He will raise the dead first and those who are left, and believe, He will gather unto Him, and we shall be taken to Heaven" explains the Preacher

"As for the wicked … the rocks and hills shall fall

on them and they will be destroyed by everlasting destruction because they did not know God and refused to believe" advises the Preacher
"The day of reckoning is at hand" adds the Preacher
Alarms are sounding all over New York city … the pending earthquake arrives, it swallows up building after building, roads open up and vehicles and people are drawn into its wake. Devastation and destruction is everywhere.
It's the beginning of the end. The countdown has begun.
Dozens of hurricanes have merged causing a vortex the size of Alaska across America.
"How long do we have?" asks Max
"I don't know" replies the Monsignor
"We've got to get above the storms" advises the Monsignor
"Maybe we can somehow, neutralise the storms" advises Max
"What will that do?" asks the Monsignor
"Buy us time" advises Max
"Time is running out, Max" advises the Monsignor
"Can we stop it?" asks the Monsignor
There is suddenly an eery quietness, then the sound of rushing water … a massive tidal wave is making its way into New York city.
Mass destruction takes place on a grand scale.
"I'm frightened" advises Max
Max and the Monsignor retreat back into the church of Saint John the Baptist.
"Steady on lass, God will not harm any of us. We are on

higher ground" advises the Monsignor
"This is hallowed ground" explains the Monsignor
The tidal wave crashes into buildings and the magnitude of the earthquake tears the city apart.
"God is here" proclaims Father McGovern
"The time of the Second Coming is at hand" advises Sister Augustine
"The Messiah has returned" replies Sister Mary
Great signs in the sky appear and a voice speaks from the clouds.
"Behold, I say unto you, believe in God, believe also in me. In my Father's house there are many mansions, if it were no so, I would not have told you. I have prepared a place for you, and I will receive you unto myself so that where I am, there you may also be" advises the voice
The voice continues to deliver it's message.
"The Kingdom of God will not be like a mustard seed … it will bear fruit seven fold" says the voice
"So I say to you, be ready, for you do not know the day or the hour when I shall be with you" concludes the voice
Max and the Monsignor decide it is time to put their plan into action.
"We may have to endure more suffering" advises the Monsignor
"God is gathering an army unto himself" replies Father McGovern
"We have nothing to fear, Father" advises the Monsignor
"God has promised that all those who believe, yet have

not seen, will be saved. He will be true to this word" advises the Monsignor

THE BLESSED TRINITY

GOD THE HOLY GHOST

Max and the Monsignor discuss their plan. The American and Russian Presidents advise both countries are on the verge of nuclear war.

Will the Holy Spirit listen?

Max and the Monsignor are in deep conversation.
"It took God only seven days to create Heaven and Earth" advises the Monsignor
"It will not take that long to destroy it" replies Max
"Are we really utterly powerless to save it?" asks Max
"There are weapons of mass destruction on the earth globally and in space, yet we are defenceless against God" explains Max
"Maybe there is a way" advises the Monsignor
"What have you got in mind, Kevin?" asks Max
"All will be revealed in time" advises the Monsignor
"God is in three persons. We call it the Blessed Trinity" explains the Monsignor
"Yes, I know of it" replies Max
"God is a supreme being, free of all sin, without stain or blemish" advises the Monsignor
"What of it?" asks Max
"Maybe if we can appeal to the Holy Spirit?" responds the Monsignor
"Just what are you planning?" asks Max
"The Holy Spirit is not an impersonal force … the Bible teaches that He is active in all our lives, a distinct person, and yet fully God" advises the Monsignor
"I know of someone who receives such messages" explains the Monsignor

"Messages from God?" asks Max
"Yes, from God, Max" advises the Monsignor
The Monsignor continues to explain to Max the significance of the messages.
"Who has received these messages?" asks Max
"A very old friend" advises the Monsignor
"Is he reliable?" asks Max
"Very reliable" advises the Monsignor
"His last message was ... What would you do if God spoke to you through His Messenger?" explains the Monsignor
"Who spoke those words, and were they an angel or God?" asks Max
"He thinks it's from an angel, but it could be from God, as in The Holy Spirit" replies the Monsignor
"Then something happened in his heart" advises the Monsignor
"What happened, Kevin?" asks Max
"God gave him the assurance, that he was renewed, in Christ" explains the Monsignor
"As in ... born again?" asks Max
"Yes, Max ... born again" advises the Monsignor
Father McGovern enters the room, and asks the Monsignor to turn on the television, for a significant announcement from the President.
"My fellow Americans, we are encountering what may be the last days.
There has been disaster, and desolation throughout the World. Famines, disease and swarms of locusts are threatening the Middle East" advises the President
"Our Generals inform me, that the Russian President,

has ordered nuclear missiles to be placed at Belarus. This is a strategic development. I have ordered our nuclear arsenal to be readied for such a response. I pray to God that day never happens" advises the President

"And so it begins" replies the Monsignor

"What begins?" asks Max

"Nation shall rise against nation" advises the Monsignor

"Kingdom shall rise against kingdom, and there shall be famines and pestilences … this is just the beginning" explains the Monsignor

"Time is of the essence, Max" advises the Monsignor

"I believe the voice that Dominic heard, was the voice of the Holy Spirit" advises the Monsignor

"I don't understand" advises Max

"Don't you see he speaks through God" explains the Monsignor

"The Holy Spirit is God, and the word of God are the words of the Holy Spirit, inspired" replies the Monsignor

"But just how do we speak to God, and how can we stop the Second Coming or the end of time?" asks Max

"I don't know the answer to that question, Max" advises the Monsignor

" … but if we can rig up some sort of communication device, maybe we can get our message across, and save the World" explains the Monsignor

"Has it ever been done before?" asks Father McGovern

"No, never" responds the Monsignor

"But it's worth a try, and it's all we've got" explains the

Monsignor

"Message, what message?" asks Max

"Leave that to me" replies the Monsignor

"What do you want us to do?" asks Father McGovern

"We need to find something we can communicate with" replies the Monsignor

"Have you any ideas, Max?" asks the Monsignor

"Maybe we can use signals, from the radar system on Earth, on a massive scale" advises Max

"A tracking device?" asks the Monsignor

"Yes, that's it … we need to find one before time runs out" advises the Monsignor

"Well, where is there such a tracking device?" asks the Monsignor

"NASA" replies Max

"Anywhere nearer, Max?" asks the Monsignor

"There's a brand new one at … One World Observatory at Freedom Tower, right here, in down town New York" advises Max

"That's it" advises the Monsignor

"And it's on hallowed ground … the World Trade Center" explains the Monsignor

"That's the answer" adds the Monsignor

"We'll have to get approval" advises Max

"How?" asks Max

"Tell them it is a mission of World importance, and that we have Papal diplomacy, and Presidential assurance" advises the Monsignor

"OK, I'm on to it, I'll get in touch with the White House immediately" advises Max

"Is there anything I can do to help?" asks Father

McGovern

"Yes, of course, Father … we will need all the help we can get to succeed" advises the Monsignor

Max and the Monsignor leave Saint John the Baptist church, jump into Max's SUV, and head straight for One World Observatory as a matter of urgency.

As they engage with various modes of traffic, a sudden newsflash on the car radio.

"We break this broadcast to announce news of a constellation over the Gobi desert in Northern China … this is the first time in over 2,000 years that the stars will appear to touch, and form a much larger star, of great magnitude … it heralds the return of The Messiah" advises the newscaster

"It's happening, all over again" advises the Monsignor

"All over again?" asks Max

"When three stars form a pattern in the celestial sphere they represent the birth or return of God to Earth" explains the Monsignor

" … and it's happening in the Gobi desert" advises the Monsignor

"It's final resting place?" asks Max

"We may find that out later" replies the Monsignor

"The star of Bethlehem?" asks Max

"Yes, it may well head to Bethlehem … the place where the prophecy was fulfilled" explains the Monsignor

The Monsignor's mobile phone begins to ring out.

"This is General Winters … I'm the Chief of staff to the President" advises the voice

"Yes, General, how can we help you?" replies the Monsignor

"I believe you and Professor Brookstein are on your way to the One World Observatory?" asks Winters

"Yes, we are close" replies the Monsignor

"The President has put me at your disposal … is there anything we can do to help?" responds Winters

"I'll hand you over to Professor Brookstein" replies the Monsignor

Max puts the call on loud speaker.

"We need to use a communication network … on a grand scale, Sir" advises Max

"Communication?" asks Winters

"It may be our only hope … and we don't have any time to waste" advises the Monsignor

"OK, I'll get everything rigged up for you … I'll advise when everything is in place" advises Winters

"Will it work?" asks Max

"It has to … the whole of civilisation is counting on it" replies the Monsignor

"When Jesus came to earth He preached in parables … His mission was peaceful, and we must reciprocate that to the word" advises the Monsignor

Max and the Monsignor eventually arrive at The One World Centre Observatory.

The Observatory is located at the top of One World Trade Center. It has dazzling panoramic views across New York and spectacular views of Manhattan.

The General, as promised, has rigged up a colossal communications device capable of incredible sound and vision.

The Monsignor's mobile phone rings.

"Are you in position?" asks the General

The Monsignor puts the call on loud speaker.

"We're inside the World Trade Center and on our way to the Observatory" advises Max

The lift eventually arrives at the Observation deck.

"OK, General, we are in position" advises the Monsignor

"We are about to link up with all other observatories around the World" advises Winter

"OK, we understand" replies Max

The General gives the order to all the other observatories. The link is set.

"OK, your good to go" advises Winters

"All we need to do is link our communications here in New York" advises Max

The star or comet has come to rest over Bethlehem, just as it did previously 2,000 years ago.

"You see Max, it's happening all over again, except this time it's proclaiming the return of The Messiah, and not the birth" explains the Monsignor

"Do you think your Irish charm will save the day?" asks Max

"I'm counting on it, Max" replies the Monsignor

All systems are on line, around the World. The Monsignor begins his address and takes the microphone in his hand.

"On behalf of all the peoples of the World, we welcome your return, and remember the wonder of your birth" advises the Monsignor

"We are not like peoples of long ago … much has changed in 2,000 years. All Nations proclaim you as their one true God" explains the Monsignor

There is no response to this message.
The Monsignor tries again in hope of a response.
"Wonderful Counsellor, Mighty God, Everlasting Father, Prince of Peace" advises the Monsignor
The Heavens begin to rumble, and the eye of God appears.
The Monsignor continues his address.
"Glorious is His Holy Name … His love will never cease. We praise our God Most High … Prince of Everlasting Peace" advises the Monsignor
"I think you've got their attention" advises Max
The whole World is listening, and communications are working flat out to televise the unfolding situation.
Suddenly, a response, a voice from the Heavens.
"My Son will return in The Second Coming, and you will glorify the Lord. After His Ascension into Heaven My Son has watched over you all. For God loved the World so much that He gave His only Son" advises the voice
"Listen to Him" explains the voice
"The day of reckoning is at hand. The time for false Messiah's and false Prophet's will be destroyed" advises the voice
A shout from all Nations proclaim …
"Christ has come"
"Christ has come"
The Monsignor continues his address, not really knowing what to say.
"We see you and the coming King in all His majesty, dressed in white. At the World's dark end those

against the Light will be slain. Our souls grow weary in this war of love" proclaims the Monsignor

Max nods to the Monsignor in agreement.

"Our Nations see no future" explains the Monsignor

The voice from the Heavens responds …

"You cannot escape the inevitable … You must all be ready" advises the voice

"All you've received will be taken from you … and God will glorify Himself in dazzling brightness. No mortal shall be able to stop the inevitable" advises the voice

"You have given yourselves more time. I will allow it, because you ask it" explains the voice

"But, the day will come, and it is close at hand. A day in Heaven is 1,000 years on Earth" advises the voice

Max asks the Monsignor to continue to negotiate on behalf of the World.

"For now, a reprieve, for all God's children" adds the voice

The Monsignor awaits instructions, but the voice advises another warning.

"Be ready, for you do not know the day or the hour, when The Son of Man will return" explains the voice.

Suddenly, the stillness returns, and the World continues on it's usual 24 hour cycle.

The President and The Pope reflect on what's happened and address all nations around the World.

Meanwhile, back in Vatican city, The Pope asks Cardinal Raphael to make contact with Monsignor O'Flaherty and Professor Brookstein.

The Monsignor's mobile phone starts to ring out.

"Your Eminence" greets the Monsignor

"I have been asked to contact you personally, by His Holiness" advises the Cardinal

"He has asked me to thank you on behalf of the whole World, and he asks that you attend an audience at the Vatican" explains Cardinal Raphael

"Yes, of course, I will, your Excellency" advises the Monsignor

"You are to be awarded the Pro Ecclesia et Pontifice decoration with Professor Brookstein" explains the Cardinal

"Thank you for such an honour" advises the Monsignor

"I am also, very grateful" advises Max

The decoration is for distinguished honour, and service at the Vatican.

"The President of the United States is also decorating both of you with their medal of honour" advises the Cardinal

This is the highest and most prestigious personal decoration awarded to those who have shown distinguished acts of valour.

"What an honour, your Eminence, both Professor Brookstein and I are deeply appreciate everything" advises the Monsignor

" … and what of the words of God, your excellency?" asks the Monsignor

"We will abide by what God says" advises the Cardinal

"On behalf of The Holy Father, thank you, for what you have both done for Rome and for the World" replies the Cardinal.

THE MILLENNIUM PRAYER
Our Father, who art in Heaven
Hallowed be thy name
Thy Kingdom come, thy will be done
On Earth as it is in Heaven
Give us this day our daily bread
And forgive those who trespass against us
And lead us not into temptation
But deliver us from evil
For thine is the Kingdom, the power and the glory
For ever and ever, Amen

In essence, and reality we are all still awaiting The Second Coming.

While the World waits, all we mortals can do is, hope and pray, that we all will be saved when that day comes!

THY WILL BE DONE

When the World begins to experience what resembles the Biblical Ten Plagues of Egypt, with outstanding consequences, The Vatican assign Monsignor Kevin O'Flaherty and Professor "Max" Brookstein to investigate on behalf of World governments.

What they find will be a Revelation to all human life on Earth, and may well cause risk to everyone and everything on the planet.

Is it an act of God or a natural phenomenon?

Do the secrets of the Bible hold the message and warning of what is really about to happen?

Could it be a natural catastrophe or a warning of The Second Coming?

Is divine guidance an option the World needs to take?

NO SCIENTIFIC EXPLANATION

The Biblical plagues of Egypt, were ten calamities inflicted by God, in order to force Pharaoh to allow the Israelites to flee from slavery.
When the Pharaoh refused Moses, God inflicted the

plagues on the Egyptians, as a divine demonstration of His power because of their disobedience.
The Egyptians worshipped false idols, and gods.
There have been many scientific discoveries, down the centuries, but when something happens in modern times without any explanation, the Vatican are asked to investigate.

Cardinal Raphael leaves the Holy Office on foot bound for a meeting with, His Holiness The Pope, at the Apostolic Palace.
The Vatican City Apostolic Palace is the official residence of The Holy Father.
It is known as the Papal Palac, and it was built in the fifth century. close to the old Saint Peter's Basilica.
The Papal Palace is closely guarded by the Swiss guards. It is the home of some official Vatican and state offices. The Palace is also home to the World famous Sistine chapel.
The Cardinal makes his way into Sala Clementina, which is a reception hall, and it is covered in magnificent and beautiful frescoes. The Papal home contains more than 1,400 rooms.
Cardinal Raphael is greeted in reception by a Vatican Papal aide.
"Bon giorno" greets the Papal aid
"Bon giorno" replies the Cardinal
"The Holy Father is awaiting your arrival, Eminence" explains the Papal aide
"Please, follow me" advises the Papal Aide
Cardinal Raphael is led into a room, which is also of

some magnificence, and there he is greeted by the Holy Father.

The Cardinal stands and waits for the Pontiff to enter the room.

"Your Holiness" greets the Cardinal

"Good morning, Cardinal Raphael. I believe there has been an outbreak of some kind in Egypt?" asks the Pontiff

"Yes, I am aware, your Holiness" replies the Cardinal

"It seems, the Governments of the World, are at the mercy of God once again" advises the Pontiff

"I think we should investigate into this matter" advises the Pontiff

"I agree Holy Father, I will assign Monsignor O'Flaherty at once" advises the Cardinal

"I too agree, he was detrimental in his last case in New York, and comes highly recommended by the American President" advises the Pontiff

"The Monsignor worked well alongside Professor Brookstein" replies the Cardinal

"I think we should engage both their expertise on this assignment too" advises the Pontiff

"I will contact Professor Brookstein directly Holy Father" responds the Cardinal

"I will keep you informed, Holy Father, of any progress concerning the investigation" advises the Cardinal

"Thank you" replies the Pontiff

Cardinal Raphael returns to his suite at the Palace of the Holy Office.

Monsignor Kevin O'Flaherty is summoned, from the Holy See, to the Cardinal's quarters.

The Cardinal greets O'Flaherty on arrival.

"Thank you for coming so quickly" advises Cardinal Raphael

"As always, I am at your disposal, Eminence" replies the Monsignor

"We seem to have a very grave situation to investigate" advises the Cardinal

"It would appear that the Nile in Egypt has turned red" explains the Cardinal

"Turned red, your Eminence?" replies the Monsignor

"Somehow, it may be of Biblical importance … an act of God" explains the Cardinal

"A natural phenomenon, with no scientific explanation" advises the Cardinal

"How can I help?" asks the Monsignor

"We have made arrangements for you to meet up with Professor Brookstein in Cairo … your work will begin there" advises the Cardinal

"What exactly are we looking for?" asks O'Flaherty

"Find out all you can concerning the phenomenon" explains the Cardinal

"World governments are in turmoil, and they are looking for answers" advises the Cardinal

"What answers are they expecting?" asks the Monsignor

"Are you aware, of the story of the Angel of Death, across the lands of Egypt?" asks the Cardinal

"I am aware of the Biblical story, yes, Eminence" replies the Monsignor

"When Moses raised Aaron's staff it struck the water, and converted it into a stream of blood" explains the

Monsignor

"That's right Monsignor, it was a sacred river" advises the Cardinal

"Begin your investigation with the River Nile and report to me your findings" advises the Cardinal

"I will begin my investigations at once, Eminence" replies O'Flaherty

The River Nile is a major river and the longest in the World.

It runs through several countries.

The Monsignor packs and leaves Vatican city. He heads for Leonardo da Vinci Airport, where he boards a plane for Cairo.

Cairo is an ancient city but also a modern metropolis and one of the biggest in the Middle East.

Professor "Max" Brookstein has flown in from John F. Kennedy International in New York. She arranges to meet the Monsignor at his hotel.

The Ramses Hilton Hotel, Cairo is situated along the Nile. It is just a short distance from Tahrir Square and the iconic Cairo Tower.

Inside Room 382, the Monsignor is unpacking, and preparing to take a shower.

A sudden knock on the door …

"Well, if it's not my old friend Max" greets the Monsignor

Max greets the Monsignor with kisses on both cheeks.

"Very European" advises the Monsignor

"Hello Monsignor, it seems we're working together again" advises Max

"Remember Max … call me Kevin" replies the

Monsignor

"Sorry, I'll remember" responds Max

"Yes, it seems so lass, we obviously make a great team" replies the Monsignor

"How do you like my room?" asks the Monsignor

"It seems to be very fitting for a Monsignor" advises Max

"Oh, it's comfortable ... but it seems ironic to be staying at the Ramses for some reason" explains the Monsignor

Suddenly, another knock at the door.

In walks a waiter with the Monsignor's dinner ...

"Thank you Mustafa" advises the Monsignor

"Would you care to join me, Max?" asks the Monsignor

"No thank you, Kevin ... I'm good to go, but I'll settle for a glass of wine" replies Max

"Coming up" replies the Monsignor

"Well, what do you know about the Nile?" asks Max

"I obviously know of the Biblical accounts but basically that's all" replies the Monsignor

" ... but I've got a feeling you and I will get to know more as we progress with our investigation" explains the Monsignor

"They are saying the Nile has turned blood red" advises Max

"What's your take on it, Max?" asks the Monsignor

"I'm thinking, somehow, it's all linked to the Biblical plagues" replies Max

The Monsignor begins to eat his meal ...

"Do you mean, the ten plagues of Egypt?" asks the Monsignor

"Yes, exactly" replies Max

"It defies all logic and explanation" advises the Monsignor

"What do you think we should do?" asks the Monsignor

"We need to take samples from the Nile, and then we can analyse the precise detail, and evaluate the reasons" replies Max

"I agree, we need some tangible evidence of what's happening" agrees the Monsignor

"We'll start our investigations tomorrow … 8am sharp" advises the Monsignor

"I'll meet you in the lobby" advises Max

"OK, Max … see you there" replies the Monsignor

Max finishes her wine and leaves the Monsignor's room.

"Oh, by the way, I'm staying here too" advises Max

"How very convenient" replies the Monsignor

Next day, the Monsignor and Max begin their investigation, and head out to Luxor, and board a canal boat.

"I've brought along sample glass containers" advises Max

"Your going to get samples as we take the cruise?" advises the Monsignor

"Yes, exactly … what better way?" replies Max

Samples are taken to be analysed for any type of contamination or explanation concerning the change of the water.

Max swiftly returns into Cairo, and begins to analyse the samples.

After a couple of hours, Max confirms that the Nile has been contaminated, and turned into a blood red environment. It is also unfit for human consumption. Max contacts the Monsignor, and updates him with her findings.

They arrange to meet again in the lobby of the Ramses Hotel.

"Well, Max, what have you found out?" asks the Monsignor

"I can confirm that it is no longer practical to drink the water out of the Nile. I agree it has been contaminated" advises Max

"Well, the authorities could have told us that" replies the Monsignor

"I've checked into the precise detail, and my observations are that it is not a hoax. We now have evidence, and written reports confirm it" advises Max

The Monsignor decides to contact the Vatican to update them with their latest investigation findings.

"Do you think it's an act of God?" asks the Monsignor

"An earthquake may be the possible cause" advises Max

"Earthquake?" asks the Monsignor

"Yes, and it could have turned the river red with it's lava flow" advises Max

"Is it a miracle or a natural catastrophe?" asks the Monsignor

"We'll have to request excavation reports to confirm" explains Max

"OK, do it, Max" advises the Monsignor

After several hours, Max returns to see the Monsignor

at his hotel with more evidence.

Max briefs the Monsignor with the new found evidence.

"It's confirmed … clues and evidence point to a natural phenomenon … no earthquakes have been reported in the area" advises Max

"No duration … it was a force of nature" explains Max

"It's all in the report, Kevin" advises Max

"No earthquake?" asks the Monsignor

"It appears to be a natural occurrence" explains Max

"I'll relay the evidence to Cardinal Raphael at once" advises the Monsignor

Several hours pass, the Cardinal informs the Pontiff of the findings, and he asks the Monsignor to stay on with Max to analyse any further investigations.

The Monsignor updates Max, and asks to look for more information.

"We've been asked to stay on, in Cairo" advises the Monsignor

"Why?" asks Max

"Cardinal Raphael asks that we dig deeper" explains the Monsignor

Max and the Monsignor begin to analyse the evidence and look for more explanations.

"In the Bible it says that man and beast suffered horrible thirst for a week" explains the Monsignor

"Surely, that is not going to happen today, Kevin?" replies Max

"What happened next?" asks Max

"A swarm of frogs was the second plague" advises the Monsignor

"Do you think that could happen again?" asks Max
"Maybe, who knows" replies the Monsignor
"The story was foretold … and it could be all happening again" adds the Monsignor
Next day, Max and the Monsignor are preparing to leave when a television news bulletin announcer, advises about an epidemic of frogs in Cairo.
"This can't be happening" advises Max
"It's nuts" adds Max
"It's happening for sure" advises the Monsignor
"But why today … in modern times?" asks Max
"I've absolutely no answer … but we'll find one Max" explains the Monsignor
"Is it a force of nature … a force of God?" asks Max
"If it is the Biblical plagues, we have another eight yet to endure … but why is it only happening in Egypt?" asks the Monsignor
A sudden NEWSFLASH …
"The World is being infested by a plague of frogs … it is an epidemic of immense proportions" advises the newsreader
"All the countries of the globe are on a warning … a surprise attack of frogs … what is causing this phenomenon to happen?" asks the newsreader
"Have we again broken our promise just like Pharaoh Ramses did in Egypt?" adds the newsreader
"Why is this happening?" asks Max
"I don't know Max … but we are surely going to find out" replies the Monsignor
"What's the answer?" asks Max
"It seems a chronology of events are taking place … we

need to look into the historical facts to find a cure, and an answer" explains the Monsignor

"How?" asks Max

"It looks as though it's following the sequence of events in the Bible, and if it does, we may be in trouble" answers the Monsignor

"What next?" asks Max

"According to the Biblical writings … the next epidemic will be of bugs" advises the Monsignor

"Bugs?" asks Max

"Yes, an infestation" explains the Monsignor

"What in Egypt?" asks Max

"Possibly, all over the World" replies the Monsignor

"Man and beast will suffer untold misery from this terrible plague" warns the Monsignor

ANOTHER NEWSFLASH APPEARS ON ALL TV CHANNELS …

"We interrupt all programmes to advise that news is coming in of an epidemic on a Worldwide scale concerning an infestation of lice and bugs … standby for further bulletins" advises the newscaster

"It's definitely following the Biblical sequence of events … when it gets to number ten I'm really in trouble" advises the Monsignor

"Why … what is the tenth plague?" asks Max

"It's not a plague, Max" advises the Monsignor

"What is it, Kevin?" asks Max

"Death of all … firstborn" explains the Monsignor

"I'm firstborn" advises the Monsignor

"Then, your in good company" replies Max

"Why, lass?" asks the Monsignor

"I'm firstborn too" advises Max

"We've got to find a cure Max … if there is one … somehow we're going to have to put the pieces of the jigsaw together" explains the Monsignor

"It's exactly like the story in the Bible" advises the Monsignor

"Except the whole World is on a collision course … and we have to somehow find an answer" advises Max

"What do you suggest, Kevin?" asks Max

"Didn't the Hebrews escape when the Angel of Death arrived by painting their doorways in sheep's blood, stopping death?" asks Max

"Yes … it's true, Max" advises the Monsignor

"The destroyer came, but passed over them" explains the Monsignor

"We must all be ready … when that day comes" advises Max

A sudden video phone call to the Monsignor is made. The Cardinal begins to update the Monsignor and Max of the Vatican's proposals.

"We have read your report" advises Cardinal Raphael

"It does seem, that we are all suffering, the pestilence, written in the Bible" explains the Cardinal

"The Holy Father asks for diligence and for prayer" advises the Cardinal

"What about the pestilence?" asks Max

The Monsignor continues his conversation with Cardinal Raphael.

"How are things in Rome, Eminence?" asks O'Flaherty

"We too are suffering in Vatican city … nowhere is free of this force of nature" advises the Cardinal

"We are working on an answer … but there is no scientific explanation to all of this" advises Max
"It seems that God has inflicted a punishment on the World" explains the Cardinal
"We all must be aware of false prophets" advises the Cardinal
"This is an international incident … it is in the air, and in the atmosphere" advises the Monsignor
"Yes, I can confirm it is air born" advises Max
"You must leave the lands of Egypt, and head to Oxford" explains the Cardinal
"Why Oxford?" asks Max
"There you will meet Professor Robert Kellerman at the Institute of Archaeology … he is well known for his teachings of ancient history and anthropology" advises the Cardinal
"Can Robert help us?" asks the Monsignor
"Professor Kellerman is a leading light in the history of the ten plagues" explains the Cardinal
"Now I see the significance of it" replies Max
"We will leave Cairo, at once, Eminence" responds the Monsignor
"May God bless you both" replies the Cardinal
The video satellite call link ends.
Max and the Monsignor leave their respective hotels and head for Cairo International Airport, where they board a plane for Heathrow, England.
They eventually arrive in Oxford, and meet Professor Kellerman.
The Professor is an Oxford academic, he is five foot ten, has blue eyes, brown hair and has a professional

look about him.

"Good afternoon, Monsignor ... I've been expecting you" greets Kellerman

"You've come with the highest of recommendations from Cardinal Raphael at the Vatican" explains Kellerman

"Well, I'm very flattered ... may I introduce my distinguished colleague, Professor Max Brookstein" advises the Monsignor

"Professor, your reputation proceeds you" greets Kellerman

"Welcome" adds the Professor

"You can call me, Max" advises Professor Brookstein

"Only if you call me, Robert" replies Kellerman

"Well, now we've got the introductions over, down to business" advises the Monsignor

"We've been watching your progress with interest ... and read your reports obviously" advises Robert

"We've also consulted various academics regarding The Torah, and the Biblical accounts" advises Robert

"... and your conclusions?" asks the Monsignor

"We confirm, this is no scientific coincidence ... and there is no modern day earthly connection to what is happening now" advises Robert

"Then it could be an act of God?" asks the Monsignor

"We have many theories ... but yes, it could be an act of God" replies Robert

"It appears the prophecies of the Bible are happening all over again" advises the Monsignor

"Yes, we believe that is true" advises Robert

"I can also confirm, and agree with that" advises Max

"The ten plagues are being cast upon the Earth again" advises Robert

"We are all looking for explanations and answers" advises the Monsignor

The Monsignor continues to advise Max and Robert about the prophecies.

"The Hebrew God inflicted the plagues, and they were designed to persuade Pharaoh to let the Israelites go" advises the Monsignor

The Monsignor continues to explain his theory.

"Moses, the son of a slave, was raised in the palace of the Pharaoh, and is said to have been chosen by God to lead the Israelites to freedom" adds the Monsignor

"Yes, we are familiar with the story" advises Robert

"But, we're not enslaved now" replies Max

"No lass, your right we're not" agrees the Monsignor

"What do you think?" asks the Monsignor

"Do you think we can find an answer to all of this Professor?" asks the Monsignor

"Is it all about freedom?" asks Max

"Maybe that's the key?" advises Robert

"I remember, in the Bible, Ramses declared … His God … is God!" advises Robert

"Then we must somehow make contact with God" replies the Monsignor

"How can we stop what's about to happen?" asks Max

"Are you firstborn, Professor Kellerman?" asks the Monsignor

"No … I am second born … why do you ask?" replies Robert

"Both Max and I are firstborn" advises the Monsignor

"And the tenth plague states that all firstborn must die" replies Max

"We must find an answer, with the utmost urgency" advises Robert

"I'll get my best team on it ... and inform all the respective governments to do the same" explains Robert

"We need answers and we need them fast" advises Max

"We have faith in you Robert" advises the Monsignor

"God be with you" replies Max

GUARDIANS OF THE AFTERLIFE ... GUARDIANS OF ALL IN THIS LIFE

A state of emergency has been declared in all countries of the World, and there is a specific find ... when ancient tablets are found in Hebrew.
Will they reveal secrets of what is happening to all human life on Earth?

"Reports are coming in from Mexico claiming that a pestilence of flies, and diseased livestock is sweeping the country" advises Max

"There has also been a claim that ancient tablets have been found in Israel, and the words written in Hebrew may hold specific clues, relevant to today, and the current pandemic sweeping the World" explains Max

"Can we obtain permission to see them?" asks the Monsignor

"We have been given official diplomatic status by all the World governments" advises Max

"We should make use of it, and it's potential" explains Max

"I agree, we must make haste, and investigate the tablets … they may hold the key to everything" replies the Monsignor

"We've had plagues four and five … now we must find the answer, before it's too late" explains the Monsignor

Max and the Monsignor drive out to a secret location in Israel.

They are given special permission, and allowed to read the Hebrew inscriptions.

Max and the Monsignor meet Doctor James Benson at an archaeological dig where the tablets were recently discovered.

"Doctor Benson?" asks the Monsignor

"I'm Benson" replies the doctor

"Good afternoon, Doctor Benson" advises the Monsignor

"Professor" greets the doctor

"No, I'm the Professor" replies Max

"Sorry … I take it your the Monsignor?" asks the

doctor
"Yes, sorry about the confusion, Professor" replies the Monsignor
"Call me James" advises the doctor
"Call me Max" replies Professor Brookstein
"Well, James, what have you found?" asks the Monsignor
"It's not what we have found, true they are really quite something" advises the doctor
"Well, what is it then?" asks the Monsignor
"The wording ... the translation" advises the doctor
"Can you translate it for us?" asks the Monsignor
"Yes, I'd be glad to" replies the doctor
Max takes out her pen and notebook to copy down the words as evidence.
The words read as follows ...
Blessed is the One who reads the words of this prophecy
Blessed are they who hear, and keep what is in it
For the time is near
"What does it mean, Kevin?" asks Max
"The end of the World ... the book of Revelation is by far the most challenging of readings in the Bible ... it foretells of the last days" replies the Monsignor
"But why do we have to endure the plagues?" asks Max
"Maybe this too is part of God's plan ... the final battle?" explains the Monsignor
"Final battle?" asks Max
"God controls the past, present and the future" advises the Monsignor
Suddenly a worker of the archaeological site shouts to

the Doctor.

"Doctor ... doctor" shouts the worker

"What is it, Marcel?" replies the doctor

"Another tablet has been found" advises Marcel

"Another tablet?" asks Max

"It could be another significant find" explains the doctor

Marcel, who is now wearing gloves, brings over the delicate artefact.

"What does the translation say?" asks the Monsignor

Doctor Benson gently lays down the artefact on a table and lightly brushes away the sand, which reveals more Hebrew words.

The Doctor relays the message to Max and the Monsignor.

"It reads as follows ...

Do not be afraid

I am the First, and the Last

I am the Living One

I am alive Forever

Do not be afraid

"It's an astonishing find" advises the Monsignor

"Indeed, we are unravelling the mysteries" explains the doctor

"Does God intend to destroy the World, Kevin?" asks Max

"There's no indication of where, and when it will happen Max" advises the Monsignor

"We need to put together everything we can find ... even the pieces of creation may need to be scrutinised" explains the Monsignor

"What do you want us to do?" asks the doctor

"Have the tablets flown by special envoy to Oxford for the attention of Professor Kellerman, as soon as possible" instructs the Monsignor

"I agree, Robert may well find out things beyond our capabilities" advises Max

The next day, government aides, and security are dispatched to England.

Max calls Robert Kellerman on the video phone.

"Have the tablets arrived, Robert?" asks Max

"Yes, I've received them under armed guard" replies Robert

"Have you been able to check if they are genuine?" asks the Monsignor

"We're using radio carbon dating techniques, and the test results should be available soon" advises Robert

"Can you let us know if they are the genuine article?" asks the Monsignor

"A careful examination will take place … we should have precise details of the archaeological find later today" explains Robert

"OK, Robert, we'll catch up with you later" advises Max

The video call ends.

Meanwhile, back in Cairo, reports are being reported on national television that an outbreak of boils on man, woman and beast is ensuing the nation.

"It's the sixth plague" advises Max

"The wording on the tablets is not of violence or threat … I just don't understand" replies the Monsignor

"It's another sign" explains the Monsignor
"But what does it mean?" asks Max
"We'll have to wait for the carbon dating results, Max" advises the Monsignor
"The World is powerless against an unknown phenomenon such as this" explains the Monsignor
"It's a plausible sequence of events" advises Max
"Just how can we stop it … it's a mystery?" explains Max
"It's definitely following the sequence in the Bible" advises the Monsignor
Another day passes, but there are still no answers as to why the World is suffering such cataclysmic events.
Then suddenly, a breakthrough … The Monsignor receives a video call from Professor Robert Kellerman in Oxford.
"Good afternoon, Kevin" advises the Professor
"Hello, Robert … do you have any news for us?" asks the Monsignor
"We've checked the carbon dating of the tablets" advises Robert
"What have you found out?" asks Max
"We concur that it is the definitive truth, and that they are an intangible treasure and genuine artefact … a thing of substance, and of real power" explains Robert
"Power?" asks the Monsignor
"They are the real thing, Kevin" adds Robert
"You said they were recently found?" asks Robert
"Yes, buried in a location for thousands of years" advises Max
"They were probably buried under secret orders"

advises the Monsignor
"I would say they are real gems and priceless" advises Robert
"It still doesn't answer why we are all being subjected to the modern day ten plagues of Egypt" advises the Monsignor
"The only logical answer is that we must follow what the Hebrews did when the tenth, and final plague occurs" answers Robert
"Then, there is no way we can stop it?" asks Max
"We will all have to take sanctuary inside Holy places and churches if we are to escape the destroyer" explains Robert
"Hallowed land may be our only hope?" asks the Monsignor
"Your Pope is safe … we must ensure that as many people of the World do the same" advises Robert
"There is no power against God" explains Robert
"No power on Earth?" asks Max
"Remember the prophecy?" advises Robert
"We need a symbol of hope" replies the Monsignor
"God is our only hope … we must put all our faith and trust in Him" explains Robert
"How do we explain this to all the countries of the World?" asks Max
"We must look for other connections, and try to find positive associations, and solutions to what may well be, the end of the World" advises Robert
"The House of God will be our sanctuary" replies the Monsignor
"We have found solid evidence, Kevin" advises Robert

"Is it a force majeure?" asks the Monsignor
"It is without doubt a superior force … a chance occurrence … a greater force, Kevin" replies Robert
"Is it sent by God?" asks Max
"There's no answer to that" advises Robert
"What we have has been rarely defined … it is related to the concept of an Act of God … an event where no one is accountable … it encompasses all human action, and reasoning" explains Robert
"Can we stop it?" asks the Monsignor
"I may have an idea, Robert" advises the Professor
"Maybe there is a way" explains Robert
"What is it Robert?" asks Max
"I'll relay it to both of you later" adds Robert
Meanwhile in the Atlantic Ocean prayers are being said on the Transatlantic Ocean Liner, Queen Mary 2 … with a warning of what's to come …
Thunder and hail on an epic scale marks the seventh plague. On board the Queen Mary 2 an SOS message has been dispatched …
Torrential rain continues all over the World. Thunder and lightening with hail and fire thrown together.
The Monsignor recalls the Book of Exodus in his Bible to Max.
EXODUS 9:16 Moses conveyed a personal message to Pharaoh from God. It said that He had purposely brought the plagues upon him, and Egypt … to show you my power, and that His Holy Name be declared throughout the whole Earth.
"We may need divine guidance, Max … to break the deadlock" advises the Monsignor

Professor Robert Kellerman contacts the Monsignor and Max by video phone.

"What have you got, Robert?" asks Max

"I may have found the answe, Max" advises Robert

"What have you found out, Robert?" asks the Monsignor

"The storm events of the seventh plague, and the tablets have links to ... The Arc of the Covenant" advises Robert

"The Arc of the Covenant?" asks the Monsignor

"Yes, an all life covenant ... that's the link" explains Robert

"I don't understand" advises Max

"Don't you see ... it's a link of great importance" answers Robert

"What are your instructions, Robert?" asks the Monsignor

"That you proceed to Mount Ararat in Turkey" advises Robert

"Why?" asks Max

"There you will find the fossilised remains of The Arc" explains Robert

"Do you mean ... Noah's Arc?" asks Max

"Yes, exactly" advises Robert

"That's it ... The House of God" replies the Monsignor

"I thought it was no more than a myth" asks Max

"No, Robert is right ... we have to keep an open mind, Max" explains the Monsignor

"OK, Robert, we agree ... we will journey to Mount Ararat, and keep you informed" advises the Monsignor

"Just what will we find there?" asks Max
"The answer" advises Robert
"The answer to what?" replies Max
"Everything" explains Robert
"I've been summoned to meet both of you on arrival, and to assist in any way I can" advises Robert
"OK, Robert, we'll keep in video contact" replies the Monsignor
"We'll see you on arrival" adds Max
The Video call ends.
Mount Ararat is snow capped, and a dormant compound volcano in the east of Turkey.
It has two major volcanic cones, and is very prominent at 11,847 feet.
This mountain is also known as The Holy Mountain, and a highlight of the World. Ascent to the summit is quite difficult mainly because of the winds, and very low temperatures.
Max and the Monsignor eventually arrive at the foot of Mount Ararat, and are joined by Professor Kellerman and a host of experienced climbers.
All are wearing protective clothing capable of withstanding freezing temperatures.
Robert greets Max and the Monsignor.
"Good morning, Max … good morning Kevin" advises the Professor
"Why are you here?" asks the Monsignor
"Like you, I am on a journey to learn more" replies Robert
"And … I was drafted in by Vatican city" explains Robert

"Yes, that figures" laughs the Monsignor
"Do you have any suspicions?" asks Max
"There are always possibilities" replies the Monsignor
"What about you, Robert?" asks Max
"We may find what we're looking for right here" replies Robert
"Let's hope so, for all our sakes" replies the Monsignor
The experienced climbers lead the way up the steep slopes of the mountain. Max, Robert and the Monsignor follow closely behind.

THE ARC OF THE COVENANT

With an air of excitement, the Monsignor, Max, and Robert begin their hazardous journey up the mountainside of Mount Ararat with their guides.
The Mountain is snow capped. and has a dormant volcano. It consists of two major volcanic cones.
"Well, Robert ... why did you decide to join us on such a hazardous expedition?" asks the Monsignor
"It was an opportunity ... too good to miss" replies Robert
"A fantastic adventure ... to go in search of the Arc" explains Robert
"Yes, I agree ... there are always possibilities Robert ... and we are on a quest to discover one of the secrets of all time, and hopefully find a solution with regards the modern day ten plagues ... and an answer to why we are experiencing them?" replies the Monsignor
"Do you think we'll find the Ark?" asks Max

"What we're hoping to find may not answer our questions, but if we take core samples, it might reveal the answer" advises Kellerman

Reflections and flickers now begin to flash on the instrument cluster equipment.

"It's a sign … are we are near?" asks the Monsignor

"Yes, it won't be in a geological instant … but the core sample can be quickly analysed, and it may well hold the key" advises Robert

A confidence is beginning to come to fruition with regards the latest findings.

Evidence of vital samples are taken by Professor Kellerman, and what he finds is a chilling revelation.

"We may well have found the lost Arc" advises Robert

" … but not as we know it" explains Robert

Robert continues to update Max, and the Monsignor.

"It's possible that the wooden structure was converted into buildings at the time … evidence is all around us … we are definitely in the right spot" advises Robert

" … and of the Arc of the Covenant?" asks the Monsignor

"The location, proof and evidence is obviously on a scale of Biblical proportions" adds Robert

"We may not find any artefacts" explains Robert

"Is it the source of the ten plagues?" asks Max

"What we have found are critical results … this is no trick" advises Robert

"It's a chilling account, but what of the ten plagues?" asks the Monsignor

Back in the United States of America all TV channels are waiting for an address from the President.

NEWSFLASH

The American President addresses the nation ...
"My fellow Americans ... the World seems to be at the mercy of mother nature ...reports are coming in of a Worldwide plague of locusts, and they are devastating all green crops ... yet another sign of God's infinite power" advises the President
"As I address you ... we have people investigating the cause, and a likely answer to all our prayers" explains the President
"God Bless you America" ends the President
Back on the summit of Mount Ararat, the Monsignor, Max and Robert continue their investigation.
News of the plague of locusts sweeping the World reaches the team.
"The eighth plague is upon us ... and the tenth draws near" advises the Monsignor
"We're beginning to run out of time to find an answer" replies Max
"Everything is happening in the order of the Egyptian plagues ... but why now ... why in this time?" asks Robert
"In truth Robert, the answer may well lie in the tenth plague ... death of the firstborn" advises the Monsignor
"Does it mean, the whole World, now?" asks Max
"I don't know ... but we may be about to find out" advises Robert
"What are your thoughts, Kevin?" asks Robert
"Back in the Bible, Pharaoh was warned, according to

the Book of Exodus" advises the Monsignor
"What warning?" asks Max
"The destroyer would go into the midst of Egypt" replies the Monsignor
"God said that all the firstborn in the land of Egypt would die … from the firstborn of Pharaoh to the firstborn of the maid servant and the firstborn of all beasts" explains the Monsignor
"How significant is it to today?" asks Max
"Very significant, Max" replies the Monsignor
"We've had deadly plagues in the recent past, the black plague being one of them … HIV/Aids being in the 1980's … it's nothing new" explains the Monsignor
"The Aids virus caused the deaths of 39 million people to date" explains the Monsignor
"It's also a known fact that today, 37 million people are living with aids" updates the Monsignor
"Yes, I see the significance" agrees Robert
"Now, we have a global epidemic. It is the fear of every man, woman and child" explains the Monsignor
"Yes … and the ease of mobility would rapidly spread disease that could wipe out populations on a massive scale" advises Max
"Tomorrow, I will contact Cardinal Raphael on the videophone, and update him concerning our investigations here on Mount Ararat" advises the Monsignor
Max, Robert and the Monsignor take to their respective beds in the tents pitched on the summit.
"It's freezing here" advises Max
"What we need is, a nip or two, to keep us warm"

advises the Monsignor

"A nip?" asks Max

The Monsignor produces a hip flask from his inside pocket.

"I think this might keep us warm" advises the Monsignor

"What's in the flask, Kevin?" asks Robert

"The finest Irish malt" replies the Monsignor

The Monsignor hands round his flask.

Max and Robert partake in the very welcome drink.

"I'll drink to your health" advises the Monsignor

"And to the success of our mission" advises Max

"I'll agree with that" replies Robert

"Second that" answers the Monsignor

Next day, the Monsignor, Max and Robert make a videophone call to Cardinal Raphael in Vatican city.

"Eminence, we have taken vital core samples at the summit of Mount Ararat" advises the Monsignor

"What have you found out?" asks the Cardinal

"We believe this may be the source of all that's happening" advises Robert

"We've also had a recent find, Monsignor" advises the Cardinal

"What have you found out?" asks the Monsignor

"Another tablet has been discovered in Italy" explains the Cardinal

"Do you think it could aid our investigation?" asks Max

Yes, and it has been confirmed that it originates over several thousands of years" explains the Cardinal

"Does it relate to the plagues, or the Arc of the

Covenant?" asks the Monsignor
"It may hold key critical results" advises the Cardinal
"How?" asks Robert
"The tablet is in Hebrew and is now being translated. It's only a recent find" explains the Cardinal
"I will advise when we have been updated concerning it's analysis" advises the Cardinal
"The Holy Father asks that you return to Rome, as soon as possible" explains the Cardinal
"I will return Eminence, when we have found positive proof and answers" replies the Monsignor
The videophone call ends.
"What will the Holy Father say?" asks Max
"I'll have to lie low for a while, Max" replies the Monsignor
A sudden newsflash from London …
"Darkness has prevailed for the last three days all over the World … this is the ninth sign or plague" advises the newscaster
The Monsignor begins to quote again from his Bible.
"And The Lord said to Moses … stretch out your hand toward Heaven, and a thick darkness covered all the land of Egypt for three days" advises the Monsignor
"And what of the tenth plague?" asks Max
"I believe it is imminent … and you and I are both firstborn" replies the Monsignor
"What can we do?" asks Max
"We'll have to take shelter" responds the Monsignor
"Where?" asks Max
"We will return to Rome … the Vatican will conceal us" explains the Monsignor

Max, Robert, and the Monsignor head back down the mountain with their guides. They all return to Rome where Cardinal Raphael greets them with some good news concerning the latest archaeological find.

Max, Robert, and the Monsignor enter the Palace of the Holy Office. An aid shows them into a very ornate room. Cardinal Raphael greets them almost immediately.

"Welcome Max, Robert and Monsignor O'Flaherty" greets the Cardinal

"We may have found an answer" advises the Cardinal

"An answer?" asks the Monsignor

"The Book of Revelation may hold the answer we are looking for" explains the Cardinal

"In what way?" asks Robert

"Have we found out what the inscription on the tablet means, Eminence?" asks the Monsignor

"Yes, it has been carefully analysed, and we believe it may hold the answer" advises the Cardinal

"What answer?" asks Max

"The inscription translates as follows … it advises that God's children must remain faithful, confident, pure and resist temptation … and that His final judgement will put an end to all evil" advises the Cardinal

"What if we can't live up to those expectations?" asks Max

"The translation also states this … I am the First, and the Last … I am the Living One" explains the Cardinal

"We have evidence of God's existence" replies the Monsignor

"How do we stop the plagues?" asks Robert
"Did you bring the sample from Mount Ararat?" asks the Cardinal
"Yes, obviously, here it is" replies Robert
"We may need that sooner than you think" adds the Cardinal
"What do you mean?" asks Max
"In the Book of Revelation it says … write down what you have seen … both the things that are now happening, and the things that will happen" informs the Cardinal
"Yes … but just how do we save the World?" asks Max
"The day of atonement is at hand" replies the Monsignor
"What is to happen was written before the foundation of the World" explains the Cardinal
"The Book of Life assures us that God will gather unto Him true followers, and take them home to Him in Heaven, when they die" replies the Monsignor
"Are we all undergoing, a kind of purification?" asks Max
"It's a chilling revelation, Monsignor" advises the Cardinal
An aid enters and whispers in the Cardinal's ear.
"I'm afraid I must leave you now … let me know if you have found any further evidence … otherwise you can find sanctuary here, in the walls of the Vatican" advises Cardinal Raphael
"Good day, Eminence" replies the Monsignor
Cardinal Raphael leaves the room.
"Very clever words … but it doesn't help us or the

World" advises Robert

"I'll get the samples from Mount Ararat analysed" advises Max

"Your both welcome to join me in my quarters for dinner" advises the Monsignor

"Our next strategic approach must be to help the peoples, and governments of the World" advises Robert

"We will begin our work tomorrow" replies the Monsignor

"But will they listen?" asks Robert

"Robert, both you and I know, it won't be easy" replies the Monsignor

Max suddenly advises that she may have found something …

"I may just have found a solution" advises Max

"Well, what is it lass?" asks the Monsignor

"I'll explain more, when I'm sure of my findings" replies Max

THE FINAL SOLUTION?

After very careful analysis, Max advises the Monsignor, and Robert that she may well have found an answer below … in the Vatican catacombs.

The Necropolis lies underneath Vatican city at varying depths below Saint Peter's Basilica.

Max meets Robert, and the Monsignor in the offices of the Holy See.

"I've been studying the detail of the archaeological tablets, and made an astonishing discovery" advises Max

"Do you think it will give us any answers, Max?" asks the Monsignor

"Yes, and you may be surprised when I tell you where the answer lies" explains Max

"Really, where?" asks Robert

"The carbon dating confirms that the source comes from below … in the Vatican catacombs" advises Max

"The catacombs?" asks the Monsignor

"How can that be" responds the Monsignor

"The tomb of Saint Peter, may hold the answer" explains Max

"Saint Peter?" asks the Monsignor

"Yes, he was the first Pope, wasn't he?" asks Max

"Yes, he was" replies the Monsignor

"The final answer may be below" explains Max

Robert asks Max about the samples from Mount Ararat.

"I think Max could be right, Kevin" replies Robert

Max updates Robert, and The Monsignor about the history of the ancient catacombs.

"Looking back into ancient history, Saint Peter's body was removed to a safer location during the barbarian invasions. When it was brought back it was buried in a different position … above the original spot, and right below the little chapel" advises Max

"Yes, that's right Max" agrees the Monsignor

"The little chapel is located below the main altar of the Basilica" explains the Monsignor

"We must make haste into the grotto's … the answer has been here, all the time" advises the Monsignor

"I will inform Cardinal Raphael of our findings, and then we will make our journey" adds the Monsignor

After advising the Cardinal … Max, Robert, and the Monsignor follow the route through the grotto, and the catacombs. They eventually find Saint Peter's tomb.

"This is it, Kevin" advises Max

"The tomb of Peter the Apostle … or Saint Peter's tomb" advises the Monsignor

Robert makes an astonishing find near the tomb.

"Look, another tablet" advises Robert

Max examines the tablet and updates Robert and the Monsignor …

"It's in Latin" advises Max

"How's your translation, Kevin?" asks Max

"Rather sketchy … but I'll do my best" replies the Monsignor

The Monsignor handles the tablet with care and begins to translate the Latin wording.

"It tells of an Angel of Revelation, claiming the final solution, and victory over the Earth" explains the Monsignor

"What else does it say?" asks Robert

"That all believers will live forever with God in perfect peace, and security. It also advises that His Kingdom will prevail, and that He will rule, and reign forever victorious" advises the Monsignor

"It also speaks of the plagues return ... but it doesn't mention the final plague, when all firstborn must die" informs the Monsignor

"Do you think it's a test?" asks Robert

"I think it's part of the plan ... and it foretells that The Second Coming is near" replies the Monsignor

"We must tell of our findings to The Holy Father, and to all the respective governments of the World" explains the Monsignor

News travels fast, that the Vatican holds the key, as to why the World is being subjected to, and experiencing the ten plagues of Egypt.

There is a new optimism that the findings will shed some light, and evidence on the current situation sweeping the World.

NEWSFLASH ACROSS THE WORLD FROM THE BBC

"Good morning ... this is the news from London" advises a newscaster

"A solution may have been found, concerning the recent outbreak of plagues which we have all been experiencing on a Worldwide scale" explains the newscaster

"Professor Maxine Brookstein and Oxford Professor, Robert Kellerman confirm carbon dated findings across the World, and below the Vatican are both linked to today's outbreak" advises the newscaster

"Saint Peter's Basilica may hold the key. Monsignor Kevin O'Flaherty of the Holy See is looking into the likelihood that everything is linked … it may well be that the World has escaped the final plague" advises the newscaster

Back at the Vatican, Max, Robert and the Monsignor are summoned to Cardinal Raphael's office in the Palace of the Holy Office.

The Cardinal addresses Max, Robert and the Monsignor.

"You have made a significant find, below under Saint Peter's Basilica" advises the Cardinal

"I have addressed the issue with The Holy Father, and he has asked me to inform you, that you will have all the support you need, and have the right reassurances around you" informs the Cardinal

"He also states, that you should not allow your confidence, to be knocked by anyone or anything, and to put your trust, and faith in yourselve" advises the Cardinal

"I would also like to say, that if you trust in your intuition, you will not need to worry about making any decisions" explains the Cardinal

"The World governments have been informed of our findings" advises the Monsignor

"They are taking comfort, that an end to the plagues, is now at hand. They have asked me to pass on their gratitude to you all, in saving the World from yet another catastrophe" advises the Cardinal

"But, we're not sure about the last remaining plague" advises the Monsignor

"We have placed all our trust in you, Monsignor" replies the Cardinal

"You have all played a vital part in the continuation of humankind and the World" explains the Cardinal

"Let that be enough" adds the Cardinal

"As for your reward" advises the Cardinal

"Our reward?" asks Max

"The American President, and the Prime Minister of the UK and all other World Leaders have decided to award you all, by making you World Ambassadors for World Peace" explains Cardinal Raphael

"It's a wonderful honour indeed, Eminence" replies the Monsignor

"Thank you … we're totally taken aback with surprise" responds Robert

"OK, what's the catch?" asks Max

"Catch?" replies the Cardinal

"Well … it does come with conditions" explains the Cardinal

"Conditions?" asks the Monsignor

"World peace is indeed a lot to take on board, Eminence" explains the Monsignor

"As Head of Investigations at the Vatican, and with Professor Brookstein, and Professor Kellerman, I wouldn't say you were untried" advises the Cardinal

"Just exactly, what do they want us to do?" asks Robert
"As I say, World Peace Keepers" responds the Cardinal
"You will be given full diplomatic status in all countries" explains the Cardinal
As the Cardinal continues to explain the fine details news of another Worldwide situation begins to unfold.
"Among the ancient ruins of Petra a further tablet has been found, and it is said to bear words relating to, The Second Coming" advises the Cardinal
"That's your next task, Monsignor" explains the Cardinal
"How can we help?" asks Max
"The city of Petra, is an archaeological seventh wonder of the World, but time is against it as it is crumbling, due to the elements" adds the Cardinal
"What do you want us to do?" asks Robert
"Seek out the Tablet, and it's findings. It may be paramount to World peace" replies Cardinal Raphael
"There's also a threat to melt the polar icecap … and in England someone is avenging themselves by murdering sex workers in the name of Mary Magdalene" advises the Cardinal
"It looks like we'll have our work cut out for us" replies Max
"It would appear so, Max" replies the Monsignor
"Robert, what is your take on it?" asks the Monsignor
"Being an Oxford scholar, I have to keep an open mind with all scientific matters" responds Robert
"And if it turns out to be unscientific?" asks Max
"The same logic applies" replies Robert

"I bid you farewell" advises the Cardinal
"Farewell?" asks Max
"We're sure to see each other again" replies the Cardinal
"And what of the Holy See?" asks Max
"Is it a law unto itself?" asks Robert
"As the Monsignor will tell you, we work in utmost secrecy, but as we are close to His Holiness The Pope … we will assist you in any way we can" replies Cardinal Raphael

THE MAGDALENE MYSTERY

When bodies are found in Cambridge and Oxford, the Police are left baffled with the graphic clues left behind.

The Vatican assign Monsignor Kevin O'Flaherty and Professor "Max" Brookstein to work alongside Oxford Professor Robert Kellerman in an attempt to find an answer.

When a mysterious woman, appears and intervenes, not only does she have "power" but also carries an age old secret, and conspiracy theory. This leads to the assumption that totally defies human logic.

Is the woman who she claims to be?

Is it a coincidence that her arrival, in Holy Week and Easter, holds more secrets and maybe the key to everything?

Does the Church know more than they claim?

As Max, Robert, and the Monsignor begin to unravel the investigation they encounter more than they bargained for, in this psychological thriller mystery.
Will the Monsignor discover why Magdalene University College in Cambridge and Oxford are both linked to the investigation?

CRYPTIC MESSAGES

Present day, Oxford and Cambridge.
It's a calm, crisp evening in Cambridge, but things start to change quickly when events take a turn for the worse in the city centre …
A couple out for an evening stroll stumble across a body near to the University campus …
The Police quickly arrive on the scene. They cordon off the area where the attack has taken place. Blue lights

and sirens can be heard around the city.

"Secure the area" shouts the Chief Inspector

"OK, what have we got here?" asks Detective Chief Inspector Victor Mallory

"A body found by a couple out for an evening walk near the River Cam, Sir" advises the young Sergeant

"Has the body been tampered with?" asks Mallory

"Yes, and we need DNA, Sir" replies the Sergeant

A sudden arrival on the scene of Doctor Mortimer (Medical Examiner) …

"I'll take over from here" advises Mortimer

"We need time of death, and all the usual information, Doctor" asks Mallory

"Yes, I'm well aware of that … you'll get, it if you leave me to do my job" responds Mortimer

"OK … soon as, Doctor" asks Mallory

"I'll be in touch, and inform you as soon as I know" explains Mortimer

Detective Chief Inspector Mallory leaves the scene, and heads back to Parkside Police Station in the centre of Cambridge.

"He seems to be on one tonight, Sergeant?" asks Mortimer

"Oh … he can be a quite touchy, Sir" replies the young Sergeant

Back at Parkside Police Station in Cambridge, Chief Superintendent, Ben Wallace, is waiting for the Chief Inspector's report.

The Chief Superintendent picks up his phone and contacts reception.

"Yes, Sir" asks the Desk Sergeant

"Has Chief Inspector Mallory reported in yet?" asks the Chief Superintendent

"He's just arrived back, Sir" replies the Desk Sergeant

"OK … have him, and his side kick report to me at once" orders the Chief Superintendent

Detective Sergeant Richard Chambers walks into the the station.

"You'd better get your skates on, the Chief Superintendent is on the warpath, asking for you, and Mallory to go to his office immediately" advises the Desk Sergeant

"OK, Bill, on my way" replies Chambers

Mallory knocks on the door of the Chief Superintendent's office and enters.

"You wanted to see me, Sir?" asks Mallory

"Yes Vic … take a seat" asks the Chief Superintendent

"Ask Sergeant Chambers to come in" advises the Chief Superintendent

Mallory gets up from his seat and shouts down the corridor.

"Chambers" shouts Mallory

"I'm here, Sir" replies Chambers

Mallory is taken aback, as Chambers is right behind him.

Both enter the Chief Superintendent's office, and close the door behind them.

"We've had Doctor Mortimer on the phone" advises the Chief Superintendent

"Has he found anything in the pathology report?" asks Mallory

"He's still working on that, but he advises that some

cryptic clues were found next to the girl's body" explains the Chief Superintendent

"Cryptic clues?" asks Chambers

"It appears that although the girl was found near the River Cam she was actually attending Magdalene College here in Cambridge" advises the Chief Superintendent

"Perhaps she was out for a stroll" adds Mallory

"Or, maybe out with friends" responds Chambers

"Neither I'm afraid … we've checked, and the college is next to the River" advises the Chief Superintendent

"What does the cryptic clue say, Sir?" asks Mallory

"It says … She became a follower of Jesus" replies the Chief Superintendent

"What does it mean, Sir?" asks Chambers

"It obviously has some religious meaning" advises Chambers

The Chief Superintendent becomes quite serious in his response.

"This may be beyond our limitations … we may need to get help on this one, Vic" advises the Chief Superintendent

"Maybe from the Church, Sir" asks Mallory

"Yes, I've spoken to my Superiors, they are looking into matters, and will update us shortly" explains the Chief Superintendent

"Was it a note that was left with the body, Sir?" asks Mallory

"No … it was a stone tablet … that's why we are checking with the church for authenticity" replies the Chief Superintendent

"A stone tablet?" asks Chambers
"Await your next instructions" advises the Chief Superintendent
Meanwhile, a call comes into the Police station of yet another body found on the campus of Oxford University, and again it is that of a young female graduate …
"They have found another one … this time in Oxford" advises Mallory
"Do you think they could be linked?" asks Chambers
"Maybe, Richard, … we'll see what forensics tell us this time" adds Mallory
A few hours later, the Chief Inspector receives a call from Doctor Mortimer.
"I've checked, and I agree that both seem to be linked … and there's another cryptic clue" advises Mortimer
"What does it say, doctor?" asks Mallory
"It's written on a tablet of stone … Sinful Woman" explains the Doctor
"Sinful?" asks Chambers
"That's a bit rich isn't it?" adds Mallory
"It signifies something … but what does it all mean" asks the Doctor
A call from the Chief Superintendent, reassures the Chief Inspector.
"We've been in contact with the Vatican, concerning the cryptic clues" advises the Chief Superintendent
"The Vatican?" replies Inspector Mallory
"The top brass, have spoken with a certain Cardinal Raphael at the Holy See, and he advises that he will send his top man to investigate on behalf of The

Vatican" explains the Chief Superintendent

"You'll have to work alongside him, Vic" advises the Chief Superintendent

"Is that an order, Sir?" asks Mallory

"It's from the top, Vic … my hands are tied" explains the Chief Superintendent

"OK, I understand … when will it happen, Sir?" asks Mallory

"In the next few days, according to our sources" advises the Chief Superintendent

"Has the press got hold of it, Sir?" asks Mallory

"There's a block on all press coverage at present, but it will soon be out in the open" advises the Chief Superintendent

"We're talking national security, Vic" explains the Chief Superintendent

"The Prime Minister has got involved … I'm afraid it's no longer a local matter" advises the Chief Superintendent

"They are likening it to a murder hunt" adds the Chief Superintendent

Back in Rome, Cardinal Raphael sends for Monsignor Kevin O'Flaherty, and he briefs him on the investigation.

"You sent for me, Eminence?" asks the Monsignor

"I did … as a matter of urgency" advises the Cardinal

"Several bodies of young women have been found in Cambridge and Oxford in England. The Prime Minister has requested our help" explains the Cardinal

"The Prime Minister of England?" asks the Monsignor

"Yes … he advises that it is a national security matter"

informs the Cardinal

"What can you tell me, Eminence?" asks the Monsignor

"Two girls bodies have been found … one in Cambridge … the other in Oxford … and there seems to be a link" explains the Cardinal

"A link … what is it, Eminence?" asks the Monsignor

"Tablets of stone were found with the bodies with a cryptic message" advises the Cardinal

"What do they say, Eminence?" asks the Monsignor

The Cardinal explains in more detail the messages on the tablets of stone.

"The first read … she became a follower of Jesus" advises the Cardinal

"And the second?" asks the Monsignor

"The second one says … Sinful Woman" explains the Cardinal

"A follower and a sinful woman … what does it mean?" asks the Monsignor

"No one knows at this time … both girls were students … one of them attended Magdalene College in Cambridge" advises the Cardinal

"Mary Magdalene … that's the link, Eminence" replies the Monsignor

"What is the Church's take on it?" asks the Monsignor

"As always, we are open minded, and neutral to all of this" explains the Cardinal

"What does the Holy Father think of this matter?" asks the Monsignor

"He asks for your presence on behalf of the British government, and to report your findings to us firstly

… before informing them" advises the Cardinal

"I fully understand, Eminence" responds the Monsignor

"We have made contact with Professor Brookstein, and she has agreed to meet you in London" advises the Cardinal

"Your flight has been booked. Please make haste and report to Chief Superintendent Ben Wallace in Cambridge, on arrival" explains the Cardinal

"Professor Brookstein will meet you at Heathrow" advises the Cardinal

"The Professor has been briefed about the investigation … you'll also report to Professor Robert Kellerman in Oxford" informs the Cardinal

"I wish you well, Monsignor … and a word of warning … the secrecy of this investigation may well be down to ancient customs and it may involve Saint Mary Magdalene … if you could tread carefully on this matter" advises the Cardinal

"As I previously advised … the Vatican must remain neutral at all times" explains the Cardinal

"I will advise you of my findings, Eminence" responds O'Flaherty

The Monsignor boards the noon flight to Heathrow from Leonardo da Vinci International Airport in Rome.

The Monsignor is met in arrivals by his old friend, Professor "Max" Brookstein.

"Hello, Max" shouts the Monsignor

Both hug and kiss each other on both cheeks.

"Welcome, Monsignor" advises Max

"Max, I've known you for so long now … call me Kevin when we're on our own" advises the Monsignor

"Yes, I will, Kevin" advises Max

Both collect the Monsignor's luggage off the merry go round, and start to walk through the arrivals terminal.

"I take it, you've read the files … and the cryptic messages?" asks Max

"Yes … no wonder the Police are baffled" replies the Monsignor

"What's your take on it?" asks Max

"The messages somehow lead to Mary Magdalene but according to The Bible, and sacred scriptures she was not the woman portrayed sinful on the day of the crucifixion" replies the Monsignor

"It's a white wash" explains the Monsignor

"A cover up by the Church?" asks Max

"I'm not sure about that, Max" replies the Monsignor

Max makes a mobile phone call to Professor Robert Kellerman in Oxford.

"Good morning, Robert" greets Max

"Hello Max … how are you" replies Robert

"I'm fine and you?" asks Max

"Very well … I take it that your phoning about the recent murders?" asks Robert

"Yes, we've been assigned by the Vatican to investigate" advises Max

"Is Monsignor O'Flaherty, with you?" asks Robert

"Yes" replies Max

"Put him on" advises Robert

"Hello Robert" replies the Monsignor

"Hello Kevin, nice to be working with you and Max again" responds Robert
"The Police have now lifted the Press blackout and they are having a field day … it's all over the news" advises Robert
"What are they saying, Robert?" asks the Monsignor
"They are calling it … the Magdalene mystery" explains Robert
"Why?" asks the Monsignor
"The tablets found beside the bodies, and the cryptic clues all lead to Mary Magdalene" advises Robert
"Do you think it's a religious ritual killing?" asks Max
"I'm not sure but I think we all need to meet up to discuss where to go next" advises the Monsignor
"OK, Robert, we'll be with you later today" advises Max
The evening news on all the TV channels portray the link to Mary Magdalene. They are also promoting all the cryptic clues to be genuine and divisive.
Meanwhile, in the ancient city of York, Nicola is watching all the news unfolding on the TV in the Christmas Angels shop in the city centre.
"My God … what's happening?" asks Nicola
"They are likening the murders to Mary Magdalene" explains Nicola
"What does it mean?" asks John Paul
"I don't know … but I must take leave and help" advises Nicola
"How can you help, Nicola?" asks John Paul
"My past may well be the link to all of this" explains Nicola

"Who is in charge of the investigation?" asks Nicola

"Turn up the TV, John Paul" asks Nicola

The News reporter begins to go into more detail, and then advises …

"We now go LIVE to Oxford, and in particular to Professor Robert Kellerman, who is in charge of the investigation …" advises the reporter

"Can you tell us what's happening, Professor?" asks the reporter

"We are currently looking into all the fine details concerning both murders with the Police, and I am also being helped by the Vatican" explains Robert

"The Vatican?" asks a reporter

"Can you give us any information concerning the appointment from the Vatican?" asks the reporter

"Monsignor Kevin O'Flaherty of the Holy See has been assigned by Cardinal Raphael together with Professor "Max" Brookstein on request by the British government" advises Robert

"We are investigating very delicate matters, and looking for answers, and a killer, at the same time" informs Robert

"What about …" asks the reporter

Suddenly, another voice enters the conversation.

"OK, that's enough for now" advises Chief Inspector Mallory

"We'll let you know, when we have more details" explains Mallory

Back in York, Nicola advises she must leave on a matter of urgency.

"I must go to Oxford, to meet this Monsignor" advises

Nicola

"Please be careful, Nicola ... remember who we really are and don't blow our cover" advises John Paul

"Peter will help look after things, while I'm away" explains Nicola

"Don't worry, John Paul ... I am needed there" advises Nicola

"Do you mean to unravel the mystery?" asks John Paul

"I may be, indeed ... the mystery" advises Nicola

Back in Oxford, "Max" and the Monsignor meet up with Robert, and confirm their suspicions.

"Are we all in agreement, that the cryptic clues, left behind, are linked to Mary Magdalene?" asks the Monsignor

"We are" reply Max and Robert

"So, we have a killer ... and a motive ... he or she must reside somewhere between Oxford and Cambridge" advises Robert

"Not necessarily" replies Max

"OK, Max ... let's have your take on the matter" asks the Monsignor

"Are we looking for a religious maniac ... and just how do we stop them?" asks Max

"We set a trap" advises the Monsignor

"How do we do it?" asks Robert

"A decoy" explains the Monsignor

"That's how we do it, Robert" adds the Monsignor

"Max will assure you, this is the only way to draw out the killer" advises the Monsignor

"Yes, it's the only way, Robert" advises Max

"I've already talked it over with the Chief Inspector,

and he agrees" informs Max

"What are the Police going to do?" asks the Monsignor

"They are lining up an officer to play the part" advises Max

Meanwhile, Nicola arrives in Cambridge, and contacts the Chief Superintendent at Parkside Police Station.

The desk Sergeant greets Nicola on arrival.

"Good afternoon. How can I help you?" asks the desk Sergeant

"I'm here to meet with the Monsignor" advises Nicola

"… and your name?" asks the desk Sergeant

"My name is Nicola … I'll only speak with the Monsignor" advises Nicola

Another voice suddenly enters the conversation.

"I'm Sergeant Chambers … I'm working on the case with Chief Inspector Mallory, we're liaising with the Monsignor, can I help you?" asks Chambers

"Tell the Monsignor, my name is Nicola Magdalena … he'll know who I am" replies Nicola

"Magdalena?" asks Chambers

"Yes, that's right … now make haste. I can help you solve this mystery" explains Nicola

"If you just wait here, I'll contact the Monsignor at once" advises Chambers

Sergeant Chambers makes a call to Chief Inspector Mallory.

"What is it, Chambers?" asks Mallory

"I think you should come into Parkside as soon as you can, Sir … and bring the Monsignor with you" explains Chambers

"Why the urgency, Sergeant?" asks Mallory

The Sergeant explains Nicola's arrival, and her name which links her to the murders.

"OK, ask her to wait, Sergeant. We'll both be there in the hour" advises Mallory

Chambers ends the phone call and turns to Nicola.

"Chief Inspector Mallory asks for you to wait here" advises Chambers

"Yes, I know what he said" replies Nicola

Chambers is stunned by Nicola's reply and wonders how she knew.

"It is of the utmost urgency if he wants to prevent more bloodshed ... I have the power to stop it" advises Nicola

RENDEZVOUS

Chief Inspector Mallory, Max, Robert, and the Monsignor head back to Parkside Police Station in Cambridge. On arrival, they encounter the mysterious Nicola.
Sergeant Chambers has asked Nicola to wait in the Chief Inspector's office.
The Chief Inspector enters his office.

"Good afternoon, I'm Chief Inspector Mallory" advises a voice
"Yes, I know who you are … and why your here" replies Nicola
"Where's the Monsignor … I asked to see the Monsignor" asks Nicola
"I am here" replies O'Flaherty
"I will only speak to you privately, Monsignor" explains Nicola

"Do you agree?" asks Nicola
"Well, yes lass ... of course I do" replies the Monsignor
Chief Inspector Mallory enters the conversation.
"You can use Interview room number 4" advises Mallory
"There must be no recording or visual photography taking place" explains Nicola
"Agreed" confirms the Monsignor
Nicola and the Monsignor leave the Chief Inspector's offic, and are shown into Interview room 4 by Sergeant Chambers.
Nicola states her case to the Monsignor.
"You said your name was Nicola, am I right?" asks the Monsignor
"Yes, Monsignor ... that is correct" replies Nicola
"And Magdalena?" asks the Monsignor
"Yes ... I am one in the same" explains Nicola
"One in the same ... sorry I don't understand" replies the Monsignor
"My real name is ... Mary of Bethany, sister of Lazarus and Martha ... I've been identified in the sacred scriptures as ... Mary Magdalene" explains Nicola
The Monsignor is stunned by Nicola's claims.
"Do you realise what you have just said?" asks the Monsignor
"Yes, I am fully aware, Monsignor ... this is real ... this is the truth" replies Nicola
"But that makes you thousands of years old" explains the Monsignor
"Yes, I am ... but what you see before you is an image ... I am an angel sent by Michael" advises Nicola

"Michael?" asks the Monsignor

"The Arch Angel" explains Nicola

"No ... this is just too good to be true" replies the Monsignor

"Nevertheless, it is all true ... and I have power" explains Nicola

"If they are recording our conversation they will hear nothing, nor see any image ... I am who I say I am" advises Nicola

"Why are you here, Nicola?" asks the Monsignor

"I am here to help you catch your killer" replies Nicola

"But, now I know your secret" advises the Monsignor

"I think my secret is safe with you" replies Nicola

"Fear not, for when I touch you, all you will remember is that I am Nicola from York, and that I will be helping you by being a decoy to catch those responsible" explains Nicola

The Chief Inspector asks Sergeant Chambers if he has managed to record anything.

"Not a word, Sir" advises Chambers

"What about visual?" asks Mallory

"Exactly the same, Sir ... nothing is working at this time" explains Chambers

"That's ridiculous" replies Mallory

Nicola advises the Monsignor of the conspiracy theory and the cover up by the Church.

"The story put out by the Church has led to a conflation of Mary of Bethany with Mary Magdalene, as well as another woman" explains Nicola

"What do you mean?" asks the Monsignor

"I am the one who anointed Jesus, but there was

another woman who was caught in adultery" advises Nicola

"So, it was someone else ... not Mary Magdalene?" asks the Monsignor

"Yes, I am sometimes called The Magdalene, and a witness to His crucifixion ... you could say it's because of secrets of The Cross" responds Nicola

"You were there?" asks the Monsignor

"I was ... and I'm here now to help you" advises Nicola

"I was a disciple of Jesus" explains Nicola

As Nicola touches the Monsignor, everything that has been discussed has been erased from his memory.

The Monsignor accepts Nicola's help in finding the killer.

"Well, Nicola ... I agree we must find a way of catching the murderer" advises the Monsignor

"I will be your decoy ... and pose as a College student to draw them out into the open" advises Nicola

"What will we do?" asks the Monsignor

"All you will have to do, is wait, I will lure them into the trap" advises Nicola

"What's in it for you, Nicola?" asks the Monsignor

"The satisfaction of finding out who is behind this, and why they are doing it ... you could say I'm Magdalena's messenger" replies Nicola

"The Cambridge College sent you?" asks the Monsignor

"I asked to come, on their behalf" explains Nicola

"I will talk to you again Monsignor, at the appropriate time" informs Nicola

Both the Monsignor, and Nicola return to confront the

others, who are waiting in the Chief Inspector's office. "We have had a detailed discussion … Nicola has decided to act as a decoy on behalf of Magdalene College" advises the Monsignor

Max updates the Monsignor on how things are progressing …

"I've been talking to Robert, and we have a plan" advises Max

"If you can incorporate it with Nicola" asks the Monsignor

"What's in it for Nicola?" asks the Chief Inspector

"Nicola has agreed to help us with catching the killer" advises the Monsignor

"… or killers?" asks Chambers

"Yes, or killers" replies the Monsignor

"We must set a trap, Inspector" advises Nicola

"How do you plan to do that?" asks Mallory

"I will work with Max, Robert, and the Monsignor … they will keep watch over me" explains Nicola

"We will be your back up" insists Mallory

"If you want to lure the suspect out into the open, that's the only way" explains Nicola

"OK, we agree Nicola … we're desperate for a result" explains Mallory

"Results and statistics … is that all you care about?" asks Robert

"We have a duty to protect everyone" explains Mallory

"You failed with regards this one, Inspector" advises the Monsignor

"It's Chief Inspector, actually" quips Mallory

"How do we know, they'll take the bait?" asks Max

"We don't … we may need several decoys to lead to Nicola" advises Mallory

"Well, Max/Robert … what's your plan?" asks the Monsignor

"We've come up with certain manoeuvres between Cambridge and Oxford" replies Max

"Manoeuvres?" asks the Monsignor

"That's right … to catch a tiger, we must spring a huge trap" advises Robert

"This is the plan …" explains Max

Addressing the evidence to hand, the plan is put into action … with Nicola at the end of it.

"Certain individuals are on our radar, and suspicion list" advises Mallory

"Are they still all out in the open, Inspector?" asks the Monsignor

"All but one are accounted for" explains Mallory

"Are we talking male or female?" asks the Monsignor

"We're talking trouble" insists Mallory

"We're not sure of their true identity" explains Mallory

"You must have some idea, Inspector?" asks Max

"The person we are looking for is known to the Police, but is as elusive as the scarlet pimpernel" replies Mallory

"We must be on our guard then" advises Robert

"If I am right this is our man or woman" replies the Monsignor

"How do we catch such a fiend?" asks Max

"With cunning observations, and divine guidance" responds Nicola

"What does she mean?" asks Mallory

"Trust me, Nicola knows exactly what she's doing" advises the Monsignor

"I have put my utmost faith in her" explains the Monsignor

"The plan must be in place tonight. We'll leak details to the press, and television channels by staging the whole thing" advises Mallory

"What will you tell them?" asks Robert

"We'll make out that we've found someone, and they are being detained … the suspect will think they are off the hook, and try again" explains Mallory

"Exactly, Chief Inspector … that's it" replies the Monsignor

"Are you sure about this, Nicola?" asks the Monsignor

"The reputation of Magdalene College rests on it as does Oxford … that's why I'm here … to bring them to justice" explains Nicola

"What if they won't stop?" asks Max

"I think my persuasive powers will convince them to do so" replies Nicola

"You see, I knew both girls … they were my friends" explains Nicola

"Do you see yourself as an avenging angel?" asks Sergeant Chambers

"I am who I am … no more, no less" replies Nicola

"We will be ready, tonight" advises Mallory

"Until tonight" responds Nicola

"Are you sure about this lass?" asks the Monsignor

"It's the only way, Monsignor" replies Nicola

Later that evening, Max, Robert, the Monsignor, and

Nicola congregate to hatch the plan.

"What makes you so sure they'll take the bait?" asks the Monsignor

"If I am sure, it is this, I suspect a certain individual at the college" advises Nicola

"Do they know you?" asks the Monsignor

"Yes, they know of me ... but they don't know my true identity" explains Nicola

"Today is Good Friday, Monsignor" states Nicola

"Yes, today is Good Friday" agrees the Monsignor

"Now is the time to put an end to what's going on" explains Nicola

"I'm no stranger to problems" explains the Monsignor

"Magdalena" asks the Monsignor

"Yes, that's my name" replies Nicola

"I must talk to you sometime" asks the Monsignor

"You can count on it, Monsignor" replies Nicola

ENTRAPMENT

It's now Easter, at Magdalene College in Cambridge. A trap has been set, and Nicola follows the same route taken by the previous victim ... but will they catch the killer?

Chief Inspector Mallory and Sergeant Chambers are in

the background with an abundance of Police officers.

"OK, Sergeant … we have to play our cards close on this one" advises Mallory

"I agree, Sir" replies Chambers

The Monsignor explains procedures to the Chief Inspector.

"You will both need to liaise closely with Nicola" advises the Monsignor

"She has a plan to draw out the suspect … then you can pounce" explains the Monsignor

"We'll have everything ready at our end, Monsignor" responds Mallory

"We have the Chief Superintendent's authority" explains Mallory

"Excellent … wait for the signal" advises the Monsignor

It's now turning dark and several decoys line the route with Nicola at the end.

"Are you ready, Nicola?" asks the Monsignor

"I am … you will of course accompany me?" asks Nicola

"Surely I will lass … everything is in place" replies the Monsignor

Max and Robert are scouting the area for clues, and checking the College for possible suspects … it's not long before something happens.

A sudden call to the Monsignor's mobile phone.

"Something's happening here" advises Max

"A man has been seen taking the same route" explains Max

The Chief inspector puts all the Police officers on

standby.

"It could, of course, be in all innocence ... but we'll see" replies the Monsignor

"We'd better check it" answers Mallory

Minutes later a man arrives on the scene walking a dog, but he is not the one they are looking for.

"Negative ... that's a negative" advises Mallory

All the Police officers reposition awaiting any movement.

"Wait ... here comes another one" advises Max

The Chief Inspector sends a message to all the Police officers.

"Be ready ... await order" insists Mallory

"Looks mighty suspicious" advises Max

"Better keep our eyes peeled, Max" advises the Monsignor

The suspect arrives on the scene, and encounters decoy number one, but passes them by.

A short walk later he comes upon decoy two but does the same thing ... he then arrives where Nicola is waiting.

"You ... it's you!" advises Nicola

"I don't know what your talking about" says the voice

"I know you, and so do my friends" explains Nicola

"What do you mean?" replies the voice

Nicola and the other two decoys are all one in the same ... Nicola is all three decoys!

"What is this?" asks the voice

"My name is Mary of Magdala" explains Nicola

"... but your Nicola at the College" replies the voice

"What you see at the college is an image. I am really,

who I say I am" replies Nicola
"Steady lass" warns the Monsignor
"What's he doing here?" asks Mallory
"Your on trial, and your life hangs in the balance" advises Nicola
"The girls you murdered were my friends" explains Nicola
"Who are you?" asks the voice, a second time
"I've told you who I am … I have the power to release you or have you crucified" warns Nicola
"She's mad" replies the voice
"She's quoting the scriptures" advises the Monsignor
"I am judge, and jury" explains Nicola
"My real name is Mary of Bethany … I am also known as Magdala … Mary of Magdalene" advises Nicola
"You are Professor James Bingham" replies Nicola
Mallory, and his officers step out from the shadows.
"I've watched your every move … the evidence against you is overwhelming" advises Nicola
"The souls of your victims cry out for revenge" explains Nicola
"You were the unseen enemy" explains Nicola
Mallory checks with Chambers.
"Are you recording this?" asks Mallory
"Every word, Sir" replies Chambers
"Let the courts deal with him, Nicola" advises the Monsignor
"I have absolute power" advises Nicola
Nicola makes a hand squeezing gesture with Bingham and it all but stops his heart.
"I can't breathe" advises Bingham

"Now, do you believe?" asks Nicola

"OK Nicola, I think he's got the message" replies the Monsignor

"Well, I wouldn't have believed it … if I hadn't seen it" adds the Monsignor

"Yes, I believe" shouts Bingham

"I wouldn't have done it … voices told me to do it" explains Bingham

"I don't believe you" replies Nicola

Chief Inspector Mallory, Chambers, Max and Robert are awaiting news.

"Shouldn't we investigate, Sir?" asks Sergeant Chambers

"No, wait for the Monsignor's signal" advises Mallory

Meanwhile, Nicola and the Monsignor agree a plan to take Bingham into custody.

"Well, Professor Bingham, are you going to come quietly?" asks the Monsignor

"I'll agree to your requests" replies Bingham

"You have no other choice" advises Nicola

"Just one question" asks the Monsignor

"Why the cryptic clues?" asks the Monsignor

"I also had my suspicions at College" advises Nicola

"I knew if I used those clues that it would answer certain questions" explains Nicola

"I'm not really from your college" advises Nicola

"Where are you from?" asks the Monsignor

"I am an angel … true and real, as you see before you … God has given me power over good, and evil" explains Nicola

"Well, have your questions been answered,

Professor?" asks the Monsignor
"Yes" replies Bingham
"I am not of this World" advises Nicola
"Your secrets safe with me, lass" advises the Monsignor
"It's one thing to have knowledge … and another thing to have wisdom" explains the Monsignor
Nicola touches his arm, and Professor Bingham only remembers the time, and the moment.
"OK, we'll get the Chief Inspector in now" advises the Monsignor
Chief Inspector Mallory arrives on the scene with his trusty Sergeant. Max and Robert also now arrive.
"You can take him away now" advises the Monsignor
"Has he confessed?" asks Mallory
"Yes, to everything" advises the Monsignor
"Where is Nicola?" asks Max
"I don't know … she was here a minute ago" replies the Monsignor
The news of catching the double murderer is all over the national newspapers, and on all television channels. Every aspect of the killer is being analysed in fine detail.

The Monsignor is preparing to leave his hotel room in Cambridge when he receives a sudden knock on the door.
"Nicola" greets the Monsignor
"Good morning, Monsignor … I wanted to catch you before you leave Cambridge" explains Nicola
"Don't worry, your secret is safe with me" advises the

Monsignor

"I know ... your a man of your word" replies Nicola

"I hope we'll meet again ... maybe if you come to York" advises Nicola

"York?" asks the Monsignor

"I am a joint owner of Christmas Angels" advises Nicola

"Christmas Angels?" asks the Monsignor

"Oh, it's an all year round shop for Christmas" explains Nicola

"Well, it sounds lovely" replies the Monsignor

"And the perfect cover" responds Nicola

"Cover?" asks the Monsignor

"Yes, my colleagues and I really are angels ... and we are watching over everyone ... come to see us" replies Nicola

"And now I must bid you farewell" advises Nicola

" ... but before I go ... ask of the Church the true facts about Mary Magdalene ... there you will find the truth" explains Nicola

With a shake of the hand, the Monsignor's memory is erased. He remembers nothing of Nicola's secret, except their conversation about the Christmas Angels shop in York, and an invitation to visit her ... plus the age old question about the true identity of Mary Magdalene, and why he must pursue everything to clear her name!

THE POWER AND THE GLORY

When ancient artefacts turn up in Israel, they are claimed by the Vatican as part of their treasures.

The archaeological finds are linked to a copper scroll at Khirbet Qumran.

They are the Dead Sea scrolls.

Monsignor Kevin O'Flaherty and Professor "Max" Brookstein are assigned by Cardinal Raphael to investigate into the works of art, but in doing so they are approached by the legendary Illuminati.

A link leads to ancient Aztec ruins for the remaining lost documents, and then to the sacred catacombs below the Vatican.

What they find may well turn into more than historical fact … and it may change the World forever!

ECHOES OF THE PAST

When the future meets the past … an ancient copper scroll turns up in Israel.
It is claimed by the Vatican as one of it's artefacts.
The scroll mentions over sixty locations with various amounts of gold and silver buried or hidden at each of site.
This is just one of 981 texts found at Khirbet Qumran … they hold a special significance as collectively they are known as, the Dead Sea scrolls.

Cardinal Raphael summons Monsignor Kevin O'Flaherty to his personal living quarters at the Palace of the Holy Office.
The Monsignor knocks on the ornate door and enters. He is greeted by an aide who advises him that the Cardinal will be with him in a matter of moments.
Another door suddenly opens in the lavishly furnished room, and Cardinal Raphael enters.
"Good morning, Eminence, you sent for me?" asks the Monsignor

The Monsignor bends on one knee and kisses the Cardinals ring.

"Good morning, Kevin. Indeed I did … what I have to discuss with you is of paramount importance, and is for your ears only" advises the Cardinal

"I am at your disposal, Eminence" answers the Monsignor

"We have recently been informed that claims have been made concerning the Dead Sea scrolls, and the Vatican" explains the Cardinal

"The Holy Father is also aware of it, and asks for you to investigate" advises the Cardinal

"You may or may not know, that we do hold part of those artefacts, here in the sacred catacombs, below the Vatican" informs the Cardinal

"No, I was not aware, Eminence … what does all of this have to do with me?" asks the Monsignor

"As I said before, we need you to locate the missing documents" advises the Cardinal

A Vatican Aide knocks on the door and enters the room.

"Ah, refreshments" advises the Cardinal

The Aide pours the tea into the ornate china cups, then bows before the Cardinal.

"Thank you Antonio" adds the Cardinal

The Aide leaves the room, and the Monsignor and Cardinal Raphael continue their detailed discussion.

"With regards the missing documents … where do I start?" asks O'Flaherty

"Your search will take you to Mexico … there you will meet up with Professor Brookstein" advises the

Cardinal

"Mexico?" replies the Monsignor

"Yes, Mexico city … Professor Brookstein is looking into the Aztec way of culture … there you will also find a link to the scrolls" explains the Cardinal

"Why Mexico, Eminence?" asks the Monsignor

"In return for Papal endorsements, and territorial rights they supported the aim of the Catholic Church, and converted to Christianity" advises the Cardinal

"Some the of the ancient Hebrew scrolls were stolen, and are believed to be in Mexico City" explains the Cardinal

"Your mission is to make contact, and return the scrolls to the Vatican" advises the Cardinal

"Now a word of warning" informs the Cardinal

"Tell no one of our meeting" explains Cardinal Raphael

"What about Max, I mean Professor Brookstein?" asks the Monsignor

"Professor Brookstein already knows, and has diplomatic anonymity" replies the Cardinal

"I'll leave at once, Eminence" assures the Monsignor

"We have made all the necessary arrangements for you to stay at The Metropolitan Cathedral of The Assumption of the Most Blessed Virgin Mary into Heaven … there you will be met by Claudio de la Concha … Professor Brookstein has been briefed" explains the Cardinal

The Monsignor gets up from his chair and kneels to kiss the Cardinal's ring.

"I will take leave of you now, Eminence, and begin my

journey" advises the Monsignor
The Monsignor makes his way to Rome International, and boards the plane bound for Mexico.
On board he meets a rather interesting character ...
The Monsignor settles back in his window seat then is greeted by another voice.
"Good afternoon, Monsignor ... I believe this is my seat" says the voice
"Good afternoon ... and you are?" asks the Monsignor
"A friend of a friend" replies the voice
"Surely man, it would be better for me to know your name, if we are to be seated next to each other, on this long journey?" asks the Monsignor
"It's better for you ... if you don't" replies the stranger
"Who are you?" asks the Monsignor
"You could say that I am an agent or a sleeper with infinite knowledge" replies the voice
"Are you Illuminati?" asks the Monsignor
"Let's just say, I have diplomatic government immunity" explains the voice
"Your Illuminati alright" replies the Monsignor
"We know who you are ... where you going ... and what your looking for" explains the voice
"Even the Vatican knows" responds O'Flaherty
The mysterious man explains what his intentions are.
"The Illuminati have existed since the dawn of time ... it's an elite organisation made up of World Leaders, business associates, and as our name states we reveal or enlighten" advises the voice
"So, your here to enlighten me ... well enlighten me then" insists the Monsignor

A lady member of the cabin crew staff looks concerned and wanders over to the Monsignor.
"Is everything alright, Sir?" asks the Stewardess
"Well, I seem to be seated next to a mystery man" answers the Monsignor
"Mystery?" asks the Stewardess
"It's alright, I'm just enlightening the Monsignor with a little banter" explains the voice
"Is that right, Sir?" asks the Stewardess
"I'll let you know, if there is a problem" answers the Monsignor
The Stewardess leaves but is still concerned regarding the other passenger.
The plane begins to taxi along the runway, and makes its ascent out of Rome International Airport.
The cabin light advises ... Unfasten Seat Belts ...
The cabin staff begin to serve lunch, and drinks to all the passengers.
"Now, where were we ... enlightenment!" asks the Monsignor
The stranger continues to put forward his case.
"What your about to embark on, will become a powerful catastrophe for the whole World" advises the voice
"Well, spit it out man ... what is it you want us to do?" asks the Monsignor
"The Dead Sea scrolls that are lost ... must remain so" advises the mystery man
"Why, what secret do they possess?" asks the Monsignor
A Steward reaches the Monsignor, and the stranger's

seats …

The Steward hands over the hot plates containing chicken, and various vegetables, with a small bottle of red wine.

The stranger continues to update the Monsignor.

"Perhaps the secrets to the end of the World. You should look below, in the sacred catacombs, for answers" advises the man

"The sacred catacombs?" asks the Monsignor

" … below the Vatican" answers the stranger

"Exactly, all the answers are there" explains the stranger

The plane begins it's descent and landing procedures are in place. It lands safely in Mexico city.

All the passengers disembark. The stranger disappears into the crowd.

The Monsignor is met by Professor "Max" Brookstein in the arrivals lounge.

"Hello, Max" advises the Monsignor

Both greet each other with a hug and kiss on both cheeks.

"Welcome, Kevin … it seems our paths have crossed again" advises Max

"What's going on, Max?" asks the Monsignor

"It appears that an emergency meeting is about to take place, and it's entering a critical phase with regards the lost artefacts" replies Max

"You know all about the Dead Sea scrolls?" asks the Monsignor

"I've been briefed by Cardinal Raphael" replies Max

"Did you have a pleasant flight, Kevin?" asks Max

"It really wasn't what I was expecting" advises the Monsignor

"Why?" asks Max

"I was interrogated ... yes that's the word ... by an agent of the Illuminati who just happened to occupy the seat next to me" explains the Monsignor

"That was not a coincidence" replies Max

"Of course it wasn't, it had all been planned ... a precariously balanced situation" advises the Monsignor

"Where's the meeting taking place, Max?" asks the Monsignor

"It's being held in one of the Federal district buildings in Mexico city ... we are both registered to attend at 3pm today" advises Max

"We'll be there, naturally ... but remember so too will the Illuminati" replies the Monsignor

"They are so powerful, and have Government Leaders at their disposal" explains the Monsignor

"Where are you staying?" asks Max

"The Vatican have arranged for me to stay at the Metropolitan Cathedral of the Assumption of the Most Blessed Virgin" replies the Monsignor

"I know it" advises Max

"I'll make my way there ... if you can meet me in an hour?" asks the Monsignor

"OK, Kevin, until then" replies Max

The Monsignor and Max go their separate ways, vowing to meet in an hour.

The Monsignor arrives by taxi at the Cathedral. It's dominance, and grandeur is there for all to see.

A young couple, obviously on vacation, ask a question of the Monsignor.

"Magnificent … such a wonderful piece of architecture" advises a voice

"Yes, I must agree with you, it is" replies the Monsignor

"I was wondering … if you wouldn't mind taking a photo for us?" asks the voice

"Of course, I'd be delighted" replies the Monsignor

The picture is taken, and the young couple move on down the street.

"Thank you" replies the voice

"Your most welcome" responds the Monsignor

The Monsignor makes his way to the main door of the Cathedral. He opens the large door and enters the Cathedral. He is met by Sister Majella.

"Good afternoon, may I help you?" asks Sister Majella

"I'm Monsignor Kevin O'Flaherty … I'm on secondment from the Vatican" replies the Monsignor

"From the Vatican?" asks Sister Majella

"Yes, that's right … Special Investigations" replies the Monsignor

"Cardinal Raphael has confirmed your arrival" advises Sister Majella

The majestic Cathedral faces south, and has two bell towers, a central domain, and three main ports. It has fifty one vaults, seventy four arches, and forty columns. Inside the Cathedral are five large altars, sixteen chapels, a choir area, corridor, and capitulary room with sacristy. It's very ornate.

The Monsignor is met by Arch Bishop Benedict

Gomez.

The Arch Bishop is a man in his late fifties, portly in stature, balding but carries an air of importance about him ...

"Good afternoon, Monsignor" advises the Arch Bishop

"Good afternoon your Excellency" replies the Monsignor

"Cardinal Raphael has advised me of your arrival, and the importance of your investigation on behalf of the Vatican" explains the Arch Bishop

"Indeed, Excellency ... I'm on an errand of mercy to look into the sacred missing Dead Sea scrolls, and Aztec culture" informs the Monsignor

"The Metropolitan Cathedral is situated on a former Aztec sacred precinct ... maybe you should start here" advises the Arch Bishop

"That is probably a good idea" replies the Monsignor

"Everything, and everyone is at your disposal ... should you require anything further, Monsignor ... remember I am always available" explains the Arch Bishop

"There is one thing I need to find out" asks the Monsignor

"What is it?" asks the Arch Bishop

"Do you know anything about the Illuminati?" asks the Monsignor

"Only of their existence ... but it is no myth that they are in operation today" replies the Arch Bishop

"Why do you ask?" asks the Arch Bishop

"I am due to attend a meeting, at the Federal Government building at 3pm" advises the Monsignor

"Well, you can be assured that the Illuminati will be there, one way or another" responds the Arch Bishop
"I bid you good day, Monsignor … until later" advises the Arch Bishop
"Excellency" replies the Monsignor
It's approaching 2pm, and Max arrives at the Cathedral to collect the Monsignor.
"I'm totally in awe of the Cathedral" advises Max
"Yes, it's truly magnificent, isn't it, Max?" replies the Monsignor
"His Excellency, the Arch Bishop informs me that it is a former Aztec site" explains the Monsignor
"We have been granted immunity" advises Max
"Do you think this is a cover up by the governments?" asks Max
"What we may find, may hold the key" replies the Monsignor
"… and of the Illuminati?" asks Max
"They remain a mystery … but like all mysteries they can be solved" advises the Monsignor
"They see … but they lack vision" explains the Monsignor
Max and the Monsignor leave the magnificence of the Cathedral, and make their way by car to the Federal Government Building. There they take their places as delegates of the Vatican.
"Are you here on behalf of The Holy See?" asks an organiser
"We are delegates of The See of Rome … The Pope" advises O'Flaherty
"Are you are here on diplomatic matters?" asks

another organiser

"Yes, exactly" replies Max

"Please take your seats ... the meeting is about to begin" advises a diplomatic aide

On the agenda is The lost Dead Sea Scrolls, their links to Israel, and to the Aztecs.

The Chair person begins to address the meeting of World delegates.

"A secret burial chamber has been found, below the Metropolitan Cathedral" advises the Chair person

"Is there anyone present investigating into this matter?" asks the Chair person

"I represent the Holy Office of the Vatican" replies the Monsignor

"And you are?" asks the Chair person

"Monsignor Kevin O'Flaherty of the Holy See" replies the Monsignor

"We've been given absolute authority, and diplomatic approval by the Vatican" explains the Monsignor

"We?" asks the Chair person

"Professor Brookstein has also been given authority by the Vatican" adds the Monsignor

"What investigation, do you mean to carry out?" asks the Chair person

"We believe that the lost scrolls of the Dead Sea are to be found here" responds the Monsignor

"You will be given every assistance, in your pursuit of the truth" advises the Chair person

"Thank you ... we hope what we find will give us the answers, we are looking for" advises the Monsignor

"Answers?" asks the Chair person

"Yes, to may be ... all of our questions" replies the Monsignor

"Motion carried ... legal and binding ... you may proceed, Monsignor" advises the Chair person

Max and the Monsignor gather their diplomatic papers together, and leave the meeting.

"Now, that's out of the way lass ... we can hopefully locate the remaining scrolls" advises the Monsignor

A team are assigned to excavate below the Metropolitan Cathedral, but it is delicate work, and it must be done slowly to preserve the architecture.

The Team Manager is updating the Monsignor on the painstaking work being carried out.

"OK, we need to minimise movement ... there are risks involved" advises Ben Shepherd, Team Manager

"Is all of this necessary, Ben?" asks the Monsignor

"Absolutely ... we are using reinforced equipment, the stone work is fragile, and we need to hold the calculated weight ... we are now entering a new, and dangerous phase" advises Ben

"It seems precariously balanced, Ben" replies the Monsignor

"We must be careful, this is critical work ... we need to stabilise the precarious stonework ... everything is a challenge" explains Ben

A worker on the site suddenly shouts to Ben ...

"I think we're in, Ben" advises the face worker

The excavation moves into another stage. They encounter another chamber. Another face worker finds a casket of some ancient origin.

What they have found is an incredible discovery.

"It appears to be an Aztec treasure" advises the face worker

"Do you think it holds the scrolls?" asks the Monsignor

The face worker brings out the casket, and hands it to the Team Manager.

Ben begins to delicately open the casket, which reveals the scrolls intact.

The missing scrolls are gently removed, and sent onward, by diplomatic envoy to the Vatican.

Some hours later, a sudden video call from Cardinal Raphael to the Monsignor requesting his imminent return to Vatican city.

"The missing scrolls have been dispatched, Eminence" advises the Monsignor

"Both you, and Professor Brookstein, need to return to Rome on the next available flight" advises the Cardinal

"What you have found, may well be crucial, to the World's existence" explains the Cardinal

The Monsignor updates the Cardinal regarding the chain of events.

"I was interrogated by the Illuminati on the plane" advises the Monsignor

"I can assure you, Monsignor, the Illuminati are a myth … they don't exist" replies the Cardinal

"With every respect, Eminence, their existence is well and truly alive" insists the Monsignor

"We will talk more, on your return, to Vatican city" replies the Cardinal

Max and the Monsignor pack and leave their respective places of stay. They head directly for Mexico

City International Airport, and board a plane for Rome International.

Both are free to go about their business, without interruption.

However, a calling card has been left on the Monsignor's seat alerting him to the fact that the Illuminati are on board the plane.

A LINK TO THE CATACOMBS

Monsignor Kevin O'Flaherty and Professor "Max" Brookstein arrive back at Rome International, and are met by Stephen, a Papal driver, and escort, to the Holy See. They encounter the Illuminati, and a chase through the streets of Rome ensues.

Stephen greets Max, and the Monsignor in the Arrivals lounge.

"Good afternoon, Monsignor" advises Stephen

"Good afternoon, Stephen" replies the Monsignor

"This is Professor Brookstein" advises the Monsignor

"Yes, I've been briefed by the Vatican" replies Stephen

"We are being pursued by the Illuminati" explains the Monsignor

"Yes, we are totally aware of the situation" responds Stephen

"May I suggest haste, Monsignor" instructs Stephen

"Yes, indeed lad … Max our lives are now in the hands of the Holy See" advises the Monsignor

Stephen escorts Max, and the Monsignor to the waiting black limousine.

The car begins it's journey through the streets of Rome.

Suddenly, Stephen notices another vehicle, following in the shadows.

"We are being followed, Monsignor" advises Stephen

"We may have to arrange a meeting party, and a diversion, Stephen" replies the Monsignor

"A diversion?" asks Max

"Yes, to deter our followers" advises the Monsignor

"Is it the Illuminati?" asks Max

"Yes, I'm afraid it is … and we need to move fast if we're going to return to the Vatican state" explains the Monsignor

"Step on it, Stephen" instructs the Monsignor

A high speed pursuit follows through the streets of Rome.

The Monsignor receives a phone call from Cardinal Raphael.

"Is everything under control, Monsignor?" asks the Cardinal

"We're being pursued by another vehicle" explains the Monsignor

"We think it is Illuminati" advises the Monsignor

"Stephen has already indicated this … we are preparing for a diversion into Vatican city" advises the Monsignor

Gun shots now start to ring out from the pursuing vehicle.

"That was a warning shot" advises Max

"They mean business" replies the Monsignor

"Don't worry, Monsignor" advises Stephen

"We're just a few streets away … and we've laid on a reception party" explains Stephen

"Good lad" replies the Monsignor

As the black limousine speeds ahead, an incendiary device goes off on the road.

"It's quite obvious they don't want us to reach our destination" advises Max

"They think we're carrying diplomatic material" replies the Monsignor

"The scrolls?" asks Max

"Yes, the scrolls" advises the Monsignor
"The Illuminati will stop at nothing to get their hands on them" explains the Monsignor
"Hold on" shouts Stephen
"Now if they will just hang on" advises Stephen
The two cars head into a side street location. Waiting to block off both exists are the Secret Police.
The Vatican limousine is waved through, leaving the pursuing car trapped.
"That's done it" advises Stephen
"Thank God for side streets, and alley ways" advises the Monsignor
"Thank God, indeed" agrees Max
"We can make our way into the Vatican grounds at ease now" replies the Monsignor
A Police escort is now in front of the black Vatican state limousine.
"We've got an escort before us" advises Stephen
"… and behind us" replies the Monsignor
The black limousine arrives safely within the Vatican grounds.
Max and The Monsignor step out of the limousine.
"Thank you, Stephen, for a most interesting ride" advises the Monsignor
The Monsignor reassures Max.
"We're safe now, Max … we have total diplomatic immunity here" advises the Monsignor
"That's very reassuring, Monsignor" replies Max
A Vatican Aide greets Max and the Monsignor on arrival.
"A meeting has been arranged with Cardinal Raphael"

advises the Monsignor

"Are we to brief him about the scrolls?" asks Max

"Yes, and their importance to the rest of the find" explains the Monsignor

"Where are they now?" asks Max

"Below in the sacred catacombs … that's the safest hiding place for them" explains the Monsignor

Max and the Monsignor enter the Palace of the Holy Office where a Papal Aide asks them to enter Cardinal Raphael's quarters.

"His Eminence will see you now" advises the Aide

A few minutes pass, then Cardinal Raphael enters the room in his robes, vestments and symbol of office.

"Good afternoon, Monsignor" greets the Cardinal

The Monsignor kneels and kisses the ring on the Cardinal's finger.

"Good afternoon, Eminence" replies the Monsignor

"Good afternoon, Professor" greets the Cardinal

Max also kneels and kisses the Cardinal's ring

"I believe, the Monsignor, has updated you about the dangers that lie ahead regarding the scrolls, Professor?" asks the Cardinal

"Yes, your Eminence, but why are they so important to the Illuminati?" asks Max

"The scrolls that are stored below the Vatican in the sacred catacombs are of no use, without the ones you found in Mexico" explains Cardinal Raphael

"You see Max, according to ancient laws and traditions, the documents are key to many treasures including Gold and Silver of significant amounts" advises the Monsignor

"I see their importance now ... and why the Illuminati are looking for it" replies Max
"It would give them incredible power over everything, and everyone" explains the Cardinal
" ... but the ancient artefacts hold a sacred secret, and curse if interrupted" advises the Cardinal
"What curse?" asks Max
"The ancient find is of significant importance ... and holds power over all" advises the Monsignor
"The Dead Sea scrolls may be more than ancient documents, and may hold the key to the end of the World" explains the Cardinal
An Aide knocks at the door, enters, and bows before the Cardinal. He leaves a tray of tea and cucumber sandwiches.
"Thank you Piotr" greets the Cardinal
"Afternoon tea" advises the Cardinal
"One of the many English customs, given to society" explains the Cardinal
"Shall I pour, Eminence?" asks O'Flaherty
"Would you be so kind?" answers the Cardinal
"Max, how do you like your tea?" asks the Monsignor
"White, no sugar, please" replies Max
"Can I tempt you both to a cucumber sandwich?" asks the Cardinal
"When in Rome" replies Max
Cardinal Raphael continues to brief Max, and the Monsignor ...
"The Holy Father has given special dispensation" advises the Cardinal
"We must make sure, that none of the documents, get

into the wrong hands" replies the Monsignor

"We believe that the Illuminati are here now" advises the Monsignor

"What, in the Vatican?" asks Max

"Precisely … they are everywhere, and that's why we must be on our guard, and prepared for every eventuality" answers the Monsignor

"Agreed, Monsignor … we must place the remaining scrolls below, in the sacred chamber" advises the Cardinal

"If the Illuminati are already here … they could make their way into the catacombs for the scrolls?" asks Max

"Yes, that's what we're hoping for … a trap will be set" advises O'Flaherty

"We can offer you complete diplomatic immunity within these walls" advises the Cardinal

"We have our own laws, and procedures" explains the Cardinal

"The Papal guard watch over the Holy Father … while the Holy See and the Secret Police watch over, everyone else" informs the Monsignor

"The Illuminati will stop at nothing to gain power" explains the Monsignor

"I agree" advises Max

Father Angelo knocks, and enters the Cardinal's quarters.

Cardinal Raphael bids the Monsignor and Max farewell and is then whisked away on other Papal business.

Max, and the Monsignor are met by Stephen, and

other members of the Holy See.

Stephen updates Max and the Monsignor with regards the continuing unfolding situation.

"Was it Illuminati following us Stephen?" asks the Monsignor

"Yes, they have been dealt with" replies Stephen

"Did you get any information out of them?" asks Max

"Only to confirm, they are agents or sleepers, employed by an unknown force" explains Stephen

"They were Illuminati, alright" replies the Monsignor

"We are at a critical stage, Stephen. Everyday is a challenge" explains the Monsignor

"I agree, Monsignor" replies Stephen

"What are your instructions?" asks Stephen

"We may need to remove the scrolls, from the Sacred Vault" advises the Monsignor

"By using a decoy?" asks Max

"The real thing won't be far away, it may be dangerous, Max" explains the Monsignor

"The Sacred Catacombs run for miles below the Vatican, no one would find you if you were lost" advises the Monsignor

"Lost?" asks Max

"Precisely, lost and maybe never to be found" explains the Monsignor

"There would be no chance of communication … cell phones are useless in the catacombs" advises Stephen

"Well, we all know the risks, and of the potential danger" replies Max

"There's always an element of risk in life, Max" replies the Monsignor

"A trap will be set then ... there must be no cover up" answers Max

"World governments may be implicated ... Heads of State are known to be members of the Illuminati" advises the Monsignor

"Our sequence of events will begin tomorrow ... if the Illuminati are in Vatican city, they will take the bait" replies Max

"The bait?" asks the Monsignor

"Only I will know it's secret ... it will draw them out into the open" replies Max

The following day arrives. The Monsignor hatches a plan to protect the Dead Sea scrolls, and draw out the imposters claiming to be Vatican officials.

Max, and the Monsignor begin to spring their surprise.

"I have my suspicions" advises the Monsignor

"Is it me?" asks Max

"Of course not, lass ... it could be one or more that we're looking for" explains the Monsignor

"Implications are very high" advises the Monsignor

"They are insiders?" advises Max

"Indeed they are, Max" replies the Monsignor

"What we find, may well turn out to be a blessing in disguise, and the World may be depending on it" explains the Monsignor

A PERILOUS SITUATION

Vatican sleuth, Monsignor Kevin O'Flaherty, and New York Professor "Max" Brookstein undertake a mission of World importance ... below the Vatican in the sacred catacombs ... to do so they join a tour guide to conceal their identities from the Illuminati.
The Vatican has several catacombs that are open to the public. The catacombs of Rome are located outside Vatican city.
Max, and the Monsignor begin to follow the tour guide into the Sacred catacombs below the Vatican.
"We'd like to take the tour of the sacred catacombs" advises the Monsignor
"How much is it?" asks Max
"It's free for the Monsignor as he is a Vatican official" advises the tour guide
"It's 50 euros for you, Madam" replies the tour guide
"The Professor is actually seconded by the Holy See, and we're on Vatican business" explains the Monsignor
The tour guide waves both of them through the

turnstiles, and they begin to take the tour.

There are 40 people on this particular tour. Max, and the Monsignor begin to mingle with the tourists.

The tour guide begins his initial explanation, and talk to the congregating tourists.

"Underneath the Vatican there are things that are sacred to Christ, and you'll see a splendid mosaic floor which is regarding the afterlife" explains the tour guide

"OK, stay with me on the walkways, and please don't stray away from our party … someone did some years ago … and they were never seen again" advises the tour guide

The tourists all laugh.

"I take it, that you meant that, as a joke?" asks a tourist

"Well, that's for you to decide" replies the tour guide

"Seriously … please stay together on this tour" explains the tour guide

Max, and the Monsignor are deep in conversation.

"I've arranged a little reception party at St Peter's tomb" advises the Monsignor

"Reception party … what is it?" asks Max

"Secrecy Max … walls have ears in the catacombs" explains the Monsignor

After walking through the catacombs for several minutes the tour guide stops near St Peter's tomb, and begins his talk again …

"This is the legendary site of the tomb of Saint Peter" advises the tour guide

"The first Pope of Rome" explains the tour guide

"As you can see it's splendour is of Vatican proportions

"... The first Pope doesn't rest alone in the Vatican tombs ... there are also many other Popes who came after Peter" advises the tour guide

The tour guide continues to explain the secrets of the catacombs.

"Peter was one of Jesus's apostles, and he was also crucified, but according to Christian tradition, Peter asked to be crucified upside down" advises the tour guide

At this point, two Vatican Aides approach the tour party.

"We are looking for Monsignor O'Flaherty" asks an aide

"I'm O'Flaherty" replies the Monsignor

"Cardinal Raphael has requested you join him in his office" advises the aide

"Let me see your papers" asks the Monsignor

One of the aides produces a gun.

"I take it, your illuminati?" asks the Monsignor

"All will be revealed" replies the aide

"Where's the reception party?" asks Max

"Let all the tour party leave ... you've found me ... let them go" asks the Monsignor

"Do we have your word, Monsignor?" asks an aide

"You have it" replies O'Flaherty

"OK, we agree ... let the others go" advises the aide

"But, Monsignor" replies Max

"Go, Max ... and find Cardinal Raphael" instructs the Monsignor

"Where are you taking me?" asks O'Flaherty

"Our orders are to take you to a secret location ... no

harm will come to you" replies the aide

The Monsignor is blind folded, then driven by car for some distance.

The Monsignor arrives at a palatial residence outside of Rome, and is brought before an old patriarch.

The Monsignor is stunned to see who is in front of him. The blindfold is removed.

"Archbishop Batalli" says a stunned Monsignor

"Yes, Monsignor" replies the Archbishop

"You are Illuminati?" asks the Monsignor

"I am … my old friend" answers the Archbishop

"I am one of the last survivors of the secret pact" explains the Archbishop

"The Illuminati" asks the Monsignor

"Yes" responds the Archbishop

"Are you aware of the underground church in Rome?" asks the Archbishop

"Below the catacombs?" asks the Monsignor

"Yes … it is called the pact of the catacombs, and it was created at the time of Vatican 2" explains the Archbishop

"Vatican 2?" asks the Monsignor

"There are lots of secrets below in the sacred catacombs … even your dead scrolls were part of the pact" informs the Archbishop

"Why am I here?" asks O'Flaherty

"You are key to the secret … what we are looking for is stored in the Vatican Library" advises the Archbishop

The Vatican Library has over two million printed books, and it's most valued documents go back, almost two thousand years.

"The Dead Sea scrolls are ancient compositions, and so are the others you found in Mexico City" explains the Archbishop

"They go back to the time of Peter … the beginning … the Word … and the Word of God" advises the Archbishop

"There are many mansions in God's House, my old friend" explains the Archbishop

"Just one question, why the secrecy … why Illuminati?" asks the Monsignor

"The Illuminati are not the ones to fear Monsignor, what remains below in the Sacred Catacombs, must remain so" instructs the Archbishop

"You'll probably never find what your looking for … the catacombs vary in depth between five and twelve metres" explains the Archbishop

"If you know all this, why the cover up … why the secrecy?" asks the Monsignor

"So many questions … but I'm afraid it all lies with His Holiness" replies the Archbishop

"The Holy Father?" replies the Monsignor

"Is He Illuminati, too?" asks O'Flaherty

"The Holy Father is protected by the Holy See, and has separate permission to hold the Holy Office in the Vatican" advises the Archbishop

"Yes, but is he Illuminati?" asks the Monsignor

"I can't answer that … there are many who are in secret … I don't know for sure" explains the Archbishop

"Why the catacombs?" asks the Monsignor

"The tomb of the dead or Saint Peter's tomb, was only

discovered in the 1940's … these are ancient Roman burial sites" replies the Archbishop

"Historical fact" answers the Monsignor

" … and what is to become of me?" asks the Monsignor

"Your free to go Monsignor. We all serve God in our own way. My way is that of ancient Vatican 2 tradition" explains the Archbishop

"The underground church" asks the Monsignor

"Yes, precisely" answers the Archbishop

"I will leave it to you Monsignor … but I have also a warning" advises the Archbishop

"What is it?" asks O'Flaherty

"There are others in the Illuminati who will stop at nothing to gain World dominance … they live in the shadows … even I am not sure who they are" warns the Archbishop

"Your secrets safe with me … and I will take your advice, but who knows what I will encounter along the way" replies the Monsignor

"If you need my assistance, Monsignor, I will help you in any way I can" advises the Archbishop.

TIME FACTOR

When the Monsignor returns to the Vatican, he has to explain why he was abducted ... will the Monsignor reveal the truth of his meeting with the Illuminati?
The Monsignor enters the Holy See offices, where he is met by an anxious Max.
"Monsignor, where have you been?" asks Max
"Yes, I've returned, lass ... no harm has been done to me" replies the Monsignor
"You're sure your OK?" asks Max
"Yes, Max ... I am OK" explains the Monsignor

"Cardinal Raphael has specifically requested you to go to his office, on your return" advises Max

"I'll go at once … Max come with me" answers the Monsignor

Max and the Monsignor make their way to the Cardinal's office in the Palace of the Holy Office.

They are both met by a Papal aide.

"The Cardinal will see you now" advises the aide

"Max, I won't be long" advises the Monsignor

The Monsignor enters the ornate room of the Holy Office where he greets Cardinal Raphael.

The Monsignor kneels and kisses the Cardinal's ring.

"Good afternoon, Eminence" greets the Monsignor

"Good afternoon, Monsignor … I've been worried about you" advises the Cardinal

"As you can see, I'm alive and well" replies the Monsignor

"… and your meeting with Archbishop Batalli?" asks the Cardinal

"You know of Archbishop Batalli?" asks the Monsignor

"We have always known he was Illuminati, and that he favours the underground Church, and Vatican 2" explains the Cardinal

"I take it, he explained why he defected?" asks the Cardinal

"Yes, he did explain, but also warned of others in the shadows" replies the Monsignor

"The sacred catacombs hold many secrets, Monsignor … the Dead Sea scrolls are only part of it" explains the Cardinal

"The Archbishop spoke of the Vatican Library,

Eminence" replies O'Flaherty

"There is also a black archive, and a secret archive. No one outside of these walls, know of it's existence" responds the Cardinal

"I knew it housed documents of philosophy, and law" answers the Monsignor

"It also holds significant writings, and historical artefacts, going back to the time of Christ and the Resurrection ... what we have, may well reveal, details of the end of the World ... and in the wrong hands, Worldwide panic would ensue" explains the Cardinal

"So, do you now see the significant importance of the Vatican in World matters, Monsignor?" asks the Cardinal

"Yes, Eminence ... I do" replies the Monsignor

"We must protect the World, from what could happen ... we are holding, what may be, a possible date, and time for the end of the World, and it's future" explains the Cardinal

"The Pontiff, is the supreme Leader, and is Christ's appointed Bishop on Earth, only he and he alone, knows the secrets of the vaults" advises the Cardinal

"What can we do?" asks O'Flaherty

"We need to create a diversion, Eminence" advises the Monsignor

"Yes, I agree, to put the Illuminati on hold" replies the Cardinal

"I have an idea, that might just work" explains the Monsignor

As Cardinal Raphael and the Monsignor continue their discussion, Max is asked by a Papal aide to attend another meeting.

The Monsignor leaves Cardinal Raphael's office and rejoins Max in the meeting room.

"Max?" asks the Monsignor

The figure turns but it's not Max, but another woman wearing a wig.

"Where is Professor Brookstein?" asks the Monsignor

"She's safe, and well for now, Monsignor" replies the voice

"Who are you?" asks the Monsignor

"An agent of the Illuminati" explains the voice

"What do you want?" asks O'Flaherty

"We are aware of your discussion with Archbishop Batalli and also with Cardinal Raphael … we want the secrets of the black vault" asks the voice

"I know of no secrets" replies the Monsignor

"Your wasting time, Monsignor … every minute you waste puts the Professor's life in danger" answers the voice

"Where is Max?" asks the Monsignor

"Why have you taken her … why are you holding her" replies the Monsignor

"I'll ask you again … tell me the secrets of the black vault" adds the voice

"I only know that it holds documents, and artefacts" responds the Monsignor

"They are of World importance … if we have them then the power, and glory will be ours to take" explains the voice

"Who are you?" asks the Monsignor

"You know who I am, who we are, and why we are

challenging everything in our path" replies the voice
"The power and the glory is God's answer to all human life ... we can't defy God" explains the Monsignor
"I have my orders" explains the voice
"... and I have mine" replies the Monsignor
"If you want to see your Professor alive again, you'll comply with our requests" replies the voice
"OK ... I'll guarantee you diplomatic immunity whilst in the Library" answers the Monsignor
"But I will have to ask permission from Cardinal Raphael" explains the Monsignor
"OK, I agree ... we will go together" answers the voice
The unknown man steps out from the shadows. The Monsignor walks a short distance to Cardinal Raphael's office. He is followed by the unknown man. The Monsignor knocks on the Cardinal's door and enters with the unknown man.
"Who are you?" asks the Cardinal
"I'm Illuminati ... we've taken the Professor hostage" replies the voice
"What do you want?" asks the Cardinal
"We want evidence of the predicted apocalypse ... we believe this is the third secret of Fatima" asks the voice
"There are no secrets" answers the Cardinal
"He's telling the truth" replies the Monsignor
Archbishop Batalli suddenly arrives on the scene.
"The Holy See are withholding the third secret" advises the Illuminati agent
"The third secret of Fatima is to remain, forever, under absolute seal" responds Cardinal Raphael
"Only The Holy Father can advise it's contents, but

even he is under orders from God" explains Raphael
Archbishop Batalli issues instructions to allow Professor Brookstein into the meeting. The Illuminati agent briefly leaves the meeting, and returns with an unharmed Professor Brookstein.
"Are you alright, Max?" asks the Monsignor
"Yes, I'm completely unharmed" replies Max
"You see, Monsignor … no harm has come to the Professor" replies Batalli
"What's going on?" asks Max
"You see, lass … we are all bound by God to keep the third secret of Fatima, for the sake of the human race" replies the Monsignor
Cardinal Raphael continues to explain why the secret needs to remain unopened.
"Cardinal Ratzinger (Pope Benedict XVI), also ordered that the third secret not be made public in order to prevent religious prophecy from being mistaken for a quest for the sensational" advises the Cardinal
"Your insistence on evidence of the predicted Apocalypse cannot be given to you or any other human beings" explains the Cardinal
The agent of the Illuminati suddenly leaves the meeting. Archbishop Batalli agrees to be interrogated by Vatican officials. The Papal guard enters and escorts Archbishop Batalli into another room
Max suddenly produces an envelope, given to her by the Illuminati.
Max hands the envelope to the Monsignor.
"What does it say, Monsignor?" asks Cardinal Raphael
"It reads … the year 5777 … the beginning of the end?"

replies the Monsignor

"What does it mean?" asks the Cardinal

"I really, have no idea, Eminence" replies the Monsignor

"I believe, that it's a prediction, out of the Book of Revelation" advises the Monsignor

"In what way?" asks the Cardinal

"It tells of the last days of abundance" advises the Monsignor

"What does 5777 mean?" asks Max

"The number 5777 is a Biblical year in Judaism. It refers to a time in the not too distant future" advises the Monsignor

"What else does it mean?" asks Max

"It means the vision of the Almighty will become a reality" explains the Monsignor

"Biblical signs from the Heavens, and it will begin sooner than later" advises the Monsignor

"You are both seconded to look into these signs immediately … May God be with you" advises Cardinal Raphael

SIGNS FROM HEAVEN

When ancient stone tablets turn up in every capital

city on Earth bearing the figures 3 and 333, it's a significant and important sign, that the World is linked to what may well be ... The Second Coming.

Monsignor Kevin O'Flaherty of the Holy See, at the Vatican, is given an envelope, which was previously handed to Professor "Max" Brookstein, from The Illuminati.
The contents of the envelope reads as follows ...

The Year 5777 ... the beginning or the end?
... but what does it all mean, and what message does it hold for the World?

Are all the signs and stories linked to the Biblical end of the World predictions or is it basically a pre-warning of what is really about to take place?

ALL WHO ARE ON THE SIDE OF TRUTH HEAR MY VOICE

THE FIRST SIGN

When Professor "Max" Brookstein is released by the Illuminati in THE POWER AND THE GLORY she hands over an envelope to the Monsignor.

It's contents read ...

THE YEAR 5777 ... THE BEGINNING AND THE END?

What does it mean, and why are other, visual and numerical signs, appearing all over the World?
"What does the number 5777 have to do with 2024?" asks the Monsignor
"It really is, very significant, Kevin" replies Max

"At sundown on 2nd October, the Jewish New Year 5777 will begin ... and The Lord's Biblical High Holy days with it" explains Max
"Amazing ... I never knew that, lass" quips the Monsignor
"It will end the Biblical Jubilee Year, this only comes round once every fifty years, which follows the Shemitah year, and that comes every seven years" replies Max
"What else does it mean, Max?" asks the Monsignor
"The fact that such a Biblical significant year (5777) is following not just a Shemitah but a Jubilee as well" explains Max
"Why the excitement?" asks the Monsignor
"It signifies what God has planned ... prophetically"

advises Max

"We must inform Cardinal Raphael, and His Holiness at once" replies the Monsignor

Max and the Monsignor arrive at the Holy Office of Cardinal Raphael in the Palace close to the Vatican.

However, the Cardinal is already in deep conversation with all the other Cardinals in the conclave.

A Papal Aide advises the Monsignor that while the meeting is in progress, the Cardinal cannot be disturbed.

"Cardinal Raphael, has left you a message, Monsignor" advises the Aide

The Monsignor reads the note out loud to Max.

"Another sign from across the World … The Tablet reads 333" advises the Monsignor

"Does Cardinal Raphael advise, where the tablet was found?" asks Max

"Dublin … Max" replies the Monsignor

"That's familiar territory for you?" asks Max

"Indeed, it is, lass" replies the Monsignor

"Then that's where we should begin our search" advises Max

Before departing for Dublin, Max and the Monsignor begin to look into the meaning and origins of 333, they are astonished by what they find.

In the Monsignor's private quarters.

"According to our investigations 333 means a union of mind, body and spirit" advises the Monsignor

"It signifies that we're all one and all things are equal" explains the Monsignor

"What else does it mean, Kevin?" asks Max

"It is also believed, when the number 333 appears, help and assistance from the extended universe is on the way" advises the Monsignor
"We must travel to Dublin, Max, to find out more of how this tablet came about" explains the Monsignor
"I'll ask for arrangements, and transportation to be carried out immediately" advises the Monsignor
"Max" and the Monsignor leave the compounds of Vatican city, and head for Leonardo da Vinci International airport on the outskirts of Rome
They enter the Departures terminal, and locate their Aer Lingus non-stop flight where the announcement is being made over the tannoy system.
"All passengers for Flight EI426 Rome to Dublin now boarding … Gate 275"
"OK, Max, that's us" advises the Monsignor
Both move along the walkways, unaware they are being followed, and enter the section for boarding, onto the aircraft.
"Good afternoon" greets the flight attendant
"Seats 12A and 12B" advises the flight attendant
"Thank you" replies Max
"Will you and your husband want adjoining seats?" asks the flight attendant
Max blushes but the Monsignor joins in the conversation.
"Hardly" replies the Monsignor
"Why?" asks the flight attendant
The Monsignor opens his black jacket to show his white collar.
"Sorry Padre, I didn't know" replies the flight

attendant

"That's alright, love ... and it's Monsignor, actually" replies O'Flaherty

The flight attendant blushes, and turns to the next passenger.

"Well, Max, that was a little bit of fun" advises the Monsignor

"I think you made their day, Kevin" advises Max

The flight takes just over three hours from Rome to Dublin.

There are no technical hitches or problems encountered on the flight.

The Aer Lingus jet arrives, more or less, on time.

"It's three fifteen local time" announces the flight attendant

"Welcome to Dublin ... we hope you have a pleasant stay" explains the flight attendant

"So do we" replies the Monsignor

"This way, Max" advises the Monsignor

Max and the Monsignor make their way, with all the other passengers, to the baggage collection area.

"This one's, mine ... here's yours Max" advises the Monsignor

Suddenly, a very familiar voice greets the Monsignor ...

"Welcome home, Kevin" advises the voice

"Father Hugh O'Connor" replies the Monsignor

"You haven't changed one bit Kevin" advises Father Hugh

"Neither have you, my old friend" replies the Monsignor

"Except, that you are now a big boy, at the Vatican" adds Father Hugh

"Hardly, Hugh ... hardly" replies the Monsignor

"May I present my associate, Max?" advises the Monsignor

"Welcome to Dublin, Max" greets Father Hugh

"Thank you for having me" replies Max

"An American" asks Father Hugh

"Be careful what you say Hugh, and don't put your foot in it like I did" advises the Monsignor

Max laughs at the Monsignor's comments ...

"Why, what happened?" asks Father Hugh

"We'll tell you all about that later" advises the Monsignor

"Max, is actually a very gifted, New York Professor" explains the Monsignor

"and your involvement with the Catholic church?" asks Father Hugh

"We are both Investigators on behalf of the Holy See. We work under the guidance of Cardinal Raphael, and the Holy Father" advises the Monsignor

Father O'Connor escorts them to Christ Church Cathedral near Temple Bar.

"It's good to be home, lass" advises the Monsignor

"Yes, I can appreciate that, Monsignor" advises Max

"Max, call me Kevin when we're together ... all the Monsignor stuff is making me nervous" explains O'Flaherty

"Are you from Dublin, Kevin?" asks Max

"I'm originally from County Cork" explains the Monsignor

"He's an adopted Son of Dublin" explains Father Hugh
The Monsignor laughs at Father Hugh's explanations …
"You'll have to try a drop of the black stuff while we're here" advises the Monsignor
"The black stuff?" asks Max
"Oh … Guinness, Max … it's World famous" explains the Monsignor
"We'll all try a wee drop later" advises Father Hugh
Max, Father Hugh, and the Monsignor take a taxi from Dublin airport and eventually arrive at Christ Church Cathedral at Temple Bar.
The Cathedral has stood at the heart of Dublin for almost a thousand years.
Many visitors, from all over the World, are welcomed at this important heritage site every day.
The Cathedral has built a reputation for having an enriched heritage throughout it's tenure of the faith. It is also celebrated for it's natural beauty, it's sense of spirituality, and generally for welcoming all generations.
"Why are we here, Hugh?" asks the Monsignor
"Did you know, you were being followed?" asks Father Hugh
"We had our suspicions" advises Max
"I've brought you here, to throw them off the scent, so to speak" advises Father Hugh
"We're actually on our way to Saint Patrick's Cathedral" explains Father Hugh
"Why all the cloak and dagger stuff?" asks Max
"Kevin and I are old hands at disguise" replies Father

Hugh
"I don't understand" replies Max
"You will, Max" replies the Monsignor
"What about the clergy here at Christ Church Cathedral?" asks Max
"They are in on it too, Kevin" replies Father Hugh
"Rather clever" advises the Monsignor
Max, Father Hugh, and the Monsignor slip out the back door to another waiting taxi that swiftly leaves and makes tracks for Saint Patrick's Cathedral, in the heart of Dublin.
"You two are like, birds of a feather" advises Max
"We ought to be, we went through the seminary together" replies Father Hugh
"Yes, brothers" advises the Monsignor
The second taxi arrives at Saint Patrick's Cathedral.
Max, Father Hug, and the Monsignor are greeted by a familiar face at the door.
"We have made arrangements for you to meet with Archbishop Cluskey shortly ... if you require anything else, just ask" advises the voice
"You'll have no problem ... I am the Dean" explains the voice
"Thank you" replies the Monsignor
"I'll wait here" advises Father Hugh
"What of the Tablet and your findings?" asks the Monsignor
"His Excellency, The Archbishop, will explain everything, shortly" advises the Dean
Archbishop Cluskey arrives ... The Monsignor kneels and kisses the Archbishop's ring. The Archbishop is in

his sixties, balding, but has a dominant demeanour.
Max and the Monsignor enter a meeting room with the Archbishop.

"Good morning, Eminence … may I present Professor Brookstein" asks the Monsignor

"Good morning to you both" replies the Archbishop

"I have recently spoken to Cardinal Raphael at the Vatican … he has asked me to advise, the other tablets you seek have turned up at most of the major capital cities in the World … they are bearing the numbers 3 and 333" explains the Archbishop

"What are your thoughts on the matter, and most of all, what have you found out?" asks the Archbishop

"We know that 3 or 333 means a connection to The Holy Trinity and God in three persons" advises the Monsignor

"We've also found out that it is also a reminder that higher spirit knowledge, ascension energy and that Divine frequency are available" explains Max

"Divine frequency?" asks the Archbishop

"A natural ability to perceive beyond the physical realm" advises the Monsignor

"Max, tell His Eminence about the note handed to you by the Illuminati" asks the Monsignor

"Are the Illuminati involved?" asks the Archbishop

"We are not sure how, Eminence … but yes they are involved" explains the Monsignor

Max begins to explain what 5777 means …

"On October 4th, 2019 … the Jewish New Year 5777 will begin. It signifies what God has planned prophetically" advises Max

"The Apocalypse?" asks the Archbishop

"Yes, Armageddon … the end of days … the end of time … the end of everything" explains Max

"Are you absolutely sure about this?" asks the Monsignor

"We can only be sure, when the day arrives" replies Max

"The name Yahweh, written in Hebrew appears as 777. The Book of Revelation says Judgements will come in three sets of 7 … seven seals, seven trumpets, seven vails or 777 judgements" explains the Monsignor

"These are the predicted prophecies" replies the Archbishop

"All the World can do, is wait" explains Max

"If it comes to fruition, His return is near" replies the Monsignor

An Aide suddenly enters the Archbishop's office and hands over a note.

"I have just received a message from Cardinal Raphael" advises the Archbishop

"It advises that the Holy Father is due to address the World" explains the Archbishop

"More Tablets have been found bearing the number 5777, stating the beginning, and the end" advises the Archbishop

Back in Vatican City, all eyes are on the Pope …

The Papal aide turns on the wide screen television.

The Pope's address is being shown on all channels in Italy.

The Holy Father begins to address the World.
"My brothers and sisters in Christ ... evidence has been found, all over the World, regarding the numbers 333 and especially the 3 secrets of Fatima. The secrets were prophesied by an apparition of The Blessed Virgin Mary. I can confirm that the third secret of Fatima is unfolding" advises the Pontiff
"Penance, Penance, Penance is now required" explains the Pontiff
The Holy Father continues to address the peoples of the World.
"There is no doomsday prediction ... we must all be strong, and put everything into The Mother of God. We must prepare ourselves ... we must entrust our lives to Christ, and to His Holy Mother ... above all we must be attentive ... very attentive, to the prayer of the rosary" explains the Pontiff
Back in Dublin it is also being debated.
"Eminent words" answers the Archbishop
"A cover up?" asks the Monsignor
"To stop Worldwide panic" explains the Archbishop
"Conspiracy theories ... biased interpretations" replies Max
"I agree, Max" replies the Monsignor
"If you would give permission for us to leave, Eminence ... we'll continue to investigate, and advise our findings to Cardinal Raphael" advises the Monsignor
"Permission granted" replies the Archbishop
Max and the Monsignor continue to look into the many signs that the World seems to be now receiving.

NATION WILL RISE AGAINST NATION

Tensions begin to mount against the super powers ... The United States, and Russia. Both countries talk of World peace, but the sheer scale of their dominance starts to impound on all other countries across the globe.

Max and the Monsignor head back to St Patrick's Cathedral in Dublin.

"We are seeing the first signs, Max" advises the Monsignor
"What does it all mean, Kevin?" asks Max
"It says in The Bible that … nation will rise against nation and kingdom against kingdom … there will be pestilence and famines, earthquakes in diverse places … all these are the beginning of sorrows" advises the Monsignor
"What happens if the United States launches a nuclear attack against Russia first?" asks Max
"Total annihilation … the last days of time" explains the Monsignor
The phone inside the Monsignor's residence begins to ring.
"Hello" answers the Monsignor
"My name is Joseph Riley … I have news of the vision of Knock, and what it means, regarding the apocalypse" advises the voice
"Where can we meet, Joseph?" asks the Monsignor
"Do you know, the Bull and Castle, in Edward Street?" asks Joseph
"You'll like it, the place has an ambience about it" explains Joseph
"What about in thirty minutes?" asks the Monsignor
Max nods her head in agreement.
"How will I recognise you?" asks the Monsignor
"I'm tall and dark" replies Joseph
"So is my Aunt" laughs the Monsignor
"OK, I'm wearing blue jeans, and a light blue shirt. I have brown hair. I'll give you my mobile number" advises Joseph

"That's more like it, lad" quips the Monsignor
"Oh … and come alone" asks Joseph
"As you wish … I understand" replies the Monsignor
"Will you be wearing your robes?" asks Joseph
"Yes, I am" replies the Monsignor
"Good … then I will easily recognise you" replies Joseph
"In half an hour then, Monsignor" advises Joseph
"Yes, I'll be there" replies the Monsignor
"Max … you'll have to shadow me to the Bull and Castle" asks the Monsignor
"OK, Kevin … don't worry, I'll be right behind you" advises Max

The Monsignor leaves the Cathedral and walks towards Lord Edward Street and eventually arrives outside at the Bull and Castle … which is a typical quaint Dublin public house.

The Monsignor is easily recognisable in his robes.

The Monsignor is greeted by the Bar Manager.

"We are honoured, Father" greets the barman
"I'm actually a Monsignor, but no pack drill in here" replies the Monsignor
"You can call me, Kevin" advises the Monsignor
"OK, what will it be, Kevin?" asks the barman
"A pint of Guinness, lad" replies the Monsignor
"Coming straight up" replies the barman

The Barman pulls a pint and hands it over to the Monsignor.

The Monsignor puts his hand in his pocket to pay for the pint.

"No, it's on the house, Kevin" explains the barman

"That's mighty generous of you, lad" replies the Monsignor
"May God Bless you" advises the Monsignor
Suddenly, another man approaches the bar.
"Are you Monsignor O'Flaherty?" asks the young man
"I am … I take it your Joseph?" asks the Monsignor
"Yes, I am" answers Joseph
"Well, I'm glad that's all out of the way" adds the Monsignor
"Now, why all the cloak and dagger stuff?" asks the Monsignor
"You can't be too careful these days" replies Joseph
"So true, Joseph" answers the Monsignor
"Oh … you can tell your friend, it's OK to join us now" advises Joseph
"How did you know?" asks the Monsignor
"I knew that you wouldn't be alone, Monsignor" replies Joseph
The Monsignor and Joseph take up a table near the window.
The Monsignor calls Max on his mobile phone and asks her to join them inside the public house.
"I'm having a black bush" advises Joseph
"I've already ordered" explains the Monsignor
Max enters the pub and takes a seat with Joseph and the Monsignor
"Joseph, this is Max … Professor Brookstein" advises the Monsignor
"Call me, Max" replies the Professor
"An American?" asks Joseph
"Steady lad, be careful what you say" adds the

Monsignor

"What are you having?" asks Joseph

"I'll have what your having" replies Max

Joseph calls the barman over to the window table.

"We'll have two black bush, please" asks Joseph

"Coming right up" replies the barman

"So, what is this about Knock, Joseph?" asks the Monsignor

"The apparition at Knock ties in with the message at Fatima, and the prophecies of the apocalypse" answers Joseph

"What does it all mean, Joseph?" asks Max

"A book written within and without, sealed with 7 seals on the right hand of Jesus. An angel proclaiming, with a loud voice, who is worthy to open the book, and to remove the seals. No one was worthy" advises Joseph

"The prophecy?" asks the Monsignor

"The Lamb of God is slain, 7 horns, 7 eyes and the 7 spirits of God sent forth to all the corners of the Earth" explains Joseph

"Well, you know your stuff, Joseph" adds the Monsignor

"More numerological warnings" replies Max

"The message of Fatima and of Knock merging as one?" asks Max

"777" replies Max

"It's another sign, Max … something is about to happen" advises the Monsignor

A sudden newsflash begins to be shown on the television in the pub.

"Can you turn the TV up please?" asks the Monsignor
The Barman obliges, and turns up the volume so everyone inside the pub can hear the newscaster.
"This is breaking news from the BBC … there has been an alleged face off between the United States and Russia … the nuclear super powers are in disagreement about various matters that are happening in the World … stay on this channel for more breaking news" advises the newscaster
"It's just beginning" explains the Monsignor
"Yes, it's a sign" replies Max
"The escalation of war between the United States and Russia could be about to happen" advises Max
"Everything as predicted … but where will it end?" asks Joseph
"In total annihilation, Joseph, total annihilation" responds the Monsignor
"Is there anything we can do?" asks Max
"Pray, Max … that both America and the Russians come to their senses … or we will all face total destruction of the human race" advises the Monsignor
"Nuclear fallout?" asks Joseph
"Yes, it will kill millions" advises Max
Mass panic sets in … everyone is running out of the pub not knowing where to go or what to do.
"Well, I've never seen a pub empty so quickly" advises the Monsignor
"What do you suggest, Kevin?" asks Max
"Shall we have one more, Joseph?" asks the Monsignor
"Why not" replies Joseph
"How about you, Max?" asks the Monsignor

"I might as well, Kevin" replies Max
"Let's make a toast to the World, and hope that the super powers can come to some arrangements" advises the Monsignor
"Can I get you something else, Father?" asks the Barman
"We'll have the same again, lad … won't you join us?" asks the Monsignor
"That's mighty fine of you … I will, Father" replies the Barman
A further announcement comes from the BBC on the big screen television.
"We interrupt this channel to advise that no treaty or truce has been made or signed by the super powers … may God be with us all in this time of need" advises the newscaster
"I'm afraid I'll have to go, Joseph" advises the Monsignor
"The inevitable, Father?" asks Joseph
"Yes, unless something can be done at the eleventh hour" replies the Monsignor
"What do you suggest, Kevin?" asks Max
"Maybe if we can convince them, one way or another, with regards the prophecies, and signs, we might just avert a global catastrophe" explains the Monsignor
"How?" asks Max
"I'll ask for us both to return to the Vatican" advises the Monsignor
"Your part of this, Max … we're in it together" explains the Monsignor
"The seals of doom are all around us … but we may

have one last chance … one last throw of the dice" advises the Monsignor

"The prophecies?" asks Joseph

"Yes, lad … and your coming too" replies the Monsignor

"It's never too late" replies Max

"Well, it may be, if we don't get our skates on" advises the Monsignor

"We need to speak to Cardinal Raphael, and His Holiness the Pope" explains the Monsignor

"The Pope can deliver … they will listen to him" advises Joseph

"Exactly, Joseph … and I'm counting on it" advises the Monsignor

"Max, we need a fast plane out of here" asks the Monsignor

"Where to … Rome?" asks Max

"No, to Washington" advises the Monsignor

"We need to persuade the American President of our aims, and to stop the confrontation with Russia, before it's too late" explains the Monsignor

THE END OF TIME?

Max, Joseph, and the Monsignor board a flight out of Dublin and head to Washington in the United States. Cardinal Raphael has the Holy Father's blessing, but is it too late?

Arrivals, Washington Dulles International Airport. The Airport is named after John Foster Dulles, who was Secretary of State under President Dwight D. Eisenhower from 1953 to 1959.

Dulles International is approximately 26 miles from Washington DC.

Max, and the Monsignor are met by Senator Jonathan Douglas.

"Sorry for the delay, Monsignor ... it's Independence Day here" advises the Senator

"Happy Independence Day" replies the Monsignor

The Senator, and the Monsignor both shake hands in greeting.

"Thank you" replies the Senator

"Do you know Professor Brookstein?" asks the Monsignor

"No we've never actually met ... but it's a pleasure" advises the Senator

"Thanks, call me Max" advises the Professor

"Thanks, Max ... I will" greets the Senator

"A fellow American?" asks the Senator

"Yes, I'm from New York" replies Max

"Your very polite, Jonathan ... this is Joseph, he's part of the team" advises the Monsignor

"Welcome to the United States, Joseph" greets the Senator

"I've been given express instructions by The Chief of Staff to take you directly for a meeting with the President" advises the Senator

"Was it sanctioned by the Vatican?" asks the Monsignor

"Sanctioned?" asks the Senator

"Sorry, Monsignor ... that's all I know" answers the Senator

Max, Joseph, and the Monsignor follow the Senator and jump into a waiting black limousine. They join a motorcade flanked with FBI Special Agents with a motorcycle escort.

After a short journey the motorcade arrives at The White House, which is the official workplace of The President of The United States.

On arrival, Senator Douglas, asks for total co-operation.

"I must ask you all to adhere to our strict security measures ... the security staff will take you in to meet the President" advises the Senator

"Thank you, Jonathan" replies the Monsignor

"I'll be at your disposal again, when you leave the meeting" explains the Senator

"Security?" asks Max

"Yes, security ... it's all part of the new regime" responds the Senator

A team/crew of two officers arrive, both are armed.

"The President has agreed to meet you all in The Oval Office" advises a Special Security Agent

"If you will please follow me?" asks the Agent

"There will be several controls to pass through … so please don't be alarmed" advises the Agent

Max, Joseph, and the Monsignor follow the security team, and are ushered into The Oval Office, where seated behind a familiar desk is the President.

"Good afternoon, Monsignor, Miss Brookstein, and …?" advises the President

"Joseph, Sir … my name is Joseph" says a very nervous voice

"For one minute, I thought you were going to say Bond" laughs the President

"Now that's really broken the ice" replies the Monsignor

"Please be seated" advises the President

"You know of the tensions between Moscow, and the US?" asks the President

"Yes, we've seen all the bulletins" replies the Monsignor

"These are trying times, for World peace" advises the President

A Presidential Aide knocks and enters the Oval Office. She whispers into the President's ear.

"Gentlemen, and Max … you may want to see this on television?" advises the President

A newscaster proclaims … "We interrupt all programmes with an update on previous bulletins …

"Italy is on full red alert … volcanoes Etna and Stromboli have violently erupted … Vesuvius is also

on the verge of eruption" advises the newscaster
"Three … that's three" advises Max
"Yes, a warning or a sign?" asks the Monsignor
"Is it from God, or have the Russians nuked Italy?" asks the President
"Italy has always been under volcanic threat … the plates run all across the country … this must be the time" explains the Monsignor
"The time?" asks the President
"The Prophecy" replies the Monsignor
"Armageddon … the Book of Revelation … the end of the World?" advises the Monsignor
"We've had tensions with Moscow" advises the President
"You both thought the same … that each one was making ready missiles for firing" explains the Monsignor
"The Volcanoes are the answer … they will be followed by earthquakes and huge tidal waves" advises the Monsignor
"What can we do?" asks the President
"Firstly, resolve the situation with Russia, make that a priority, Mr. President" advises the Monsignor
"Then advise them that it is all down to eruptions, and ask them to stand down" explains the Monsignor
The President calls in a Whitehouse Aide issuing an urgent connection to Moscow.
"Get the Russian President on the phone" orders the President
As the President begins to calm the situation, Max, Joseph and the Monsignor contact the Vatican for an

update.

"You can make your call in another office" advises the Chief of Staff

The Monsignor, Max and Joseph take a "video" call from Cardinal Raphael

"Good afternoon, Eminence" greets the Monsignor

"Good afternoon, Monsignor" replies Cardinal Raphael

"I have had a meeting with the Holy Father … I take it that you are aware of the situation here, and the shift in the seismic plates?" asks the Cardinal

"Yes, Eminence" replies O'Flaherty

"Have you briefed the President?" asks the Cardinal

"Yes, he is actually on the phone, right now, to the Russian President in Moscow" explains the Monsignor

"More signs are appearing in the sky, and everyone is asking the same question … Is this the end of the World?" advises the Cardinal

"We have informed everyone regarding the prophecies and the possible outcome … all we can do is wait" advises the Monsignor

"If you can take the next available flight out of Washington for Rome … we will await your imminent return to Vatican City" requests Cardinal Raphael

"We will all depart Washington, shortly" replies the Monsignor

"We?" asks the Cardinal

"The Professor and Joseph" explains the Monsignor

"Yes, you will need diplomatic clearance" advises the Cardinal

"I'm sure the President will clear that" replies the

Monsignor

"OK, call when your in flight" asks Cardinal Raphael

"If you or we have any further news we'll discuss it then … I wish you a good journey" advises the Cardinal

Max, Joseph and the Monsignor are escorted by the Chief of Staff back into the Oval Office, where American President, James Denver begins to update them concerning his call with the Russian President.

"I have just spoken, with my counterpart, the Russian President in Moscow. I have managed to persuade him, that it is all down to volcanic and earthquake eruptions. He has acknowledged our concerns, and accepted our proposal" advises the President

"Proposal?" asks the Chief of Staff

"We have agreed to postpone any talk of armament at this present time" explains the President

"Excellent" replies the Monsignor

"Forgive me … have you contacted the Vatican?" asks the President

"Yes, I have made contact, and we have been instructed to return to Vatican city as soon as possible … can you grant diplomatic clearance?" asks the Monsignor

"Granted … I have a letter for His Holiness, The Pope … if you could take it in the diplomatic bag?" asks the President

"It would be an honour, Mr President" replies the Monsignor

"The Chief of Staff will arrange for an escort to Washington DC Airport and special clearance on

behalf of The White House" explains the President
"Thank you, Mr President ... that's very kind" replies the Monsignor
"Well, Max ... have you anything to ask of me?" asks the President
"Only for your help in striving for World peace" replies Max
"You have it ... if I can help any of you at all, please let me know" responds the President
After the various hand shakes, Max, Joseph and the Monsignor leave the Oval Room and follow the Chief of Staff out of the Whitehouse into a waiting black limousine.
"We've laid on a special escort all the way to the airport" advises the Chief of Staff
"Your cleared to go" explains the Chief of Staff
The journey to the airport takes twenty minutes. Special clearance via the Presidential gate. The plane is now boarding for Rome.
"Now all we have to do is arrive safely in Rome" advises the Monsignor
"I agree, what possibly could go wrong?" replies Max
"I've got a feeling ... this flight could hold some answers" explains the Monsignor

BLESSED BE GOD, FOREVER

Max, Joseph, and the Monsignor board the Virgin transatlantic flight bound for Rome International at Washington Dulles airport. They are unaware of the complications that lie ahead on board the flight.
"It was nice of the President to see us, and we have first class seats" advises Joseph
"I hope your not blinded by gestures of grand illusions, lad" replies the Monsignor
"No … not at all" replies Joseph
"Max, what did you think of our meeting?" asks the Monsignor
"Everyone was kind and diplomatic … just what I expected, Kevin" replies Max

The Captain makes a sudden announcement to the passengers.
"We are just an hour away from Rome International … but we have to make an emergency landing" advises the Captain
"That sounds serious" replies the Monsignor
The Captain continues his announcement to the passengers …
"We believe that a power bank is causing concern in the holding area … we may have to divert … we will keep you all updated on the situation" explains the Captain
"I don't like the sound of that" advises Max
"Terrorists?" asks Joseph
"Who knows … they are being very coy, Joseph" advises the Monsignor
"Is it another sign, Kevin?" asks Max
"I don't think so … do you?" replies the Monsignor
"It's hard to tell" replies Max
"What do you think, Joseph?" asks the Monsignor
"We've had no sign … but who knows what it means" replies Joseph
The flight attendants begin to mingle among the passengers.
"Would you all like a complimentary drink?" asks a flight attendant
"We would lass … especially as it's free" replies the Monsignor
"What would you like, Father?" asks the attendant
"I'll have a Guinness" replies the Monsignor
"Sorry, we only have spirits, Father" replies the

attendant

"OK, under the circumstances … a small whiskey" advises the Monsignor

"Are you Irish?" asks the attendant

"Got it, in one" replies the Monsignor

"Are you a Bishop?" asks the attendant

"No … only a lowly Monsignor" replies O'Flaherty

"What will your friends, have?" asks the attendant

"I'll have a bourbon" replies Max

"Brandy for me" answers Joseph

"Well, that's well oiled our spirits … if you'll pardon the pun" replies the Monsignor

The Captain makes another announcement advising that the plane is shortly landing at Rome International.

"Please fasten all safety belts … we have been cleared for an emergency landing" advises the Captain

"Time to say our prayers, Monsignor?" asks Joseph

"You say them lad … I'll have another whiskey" replies the Monsignor

The plane lands safely after the power bank breach in the holding area.

The Captain makes a further announcement to all passengers.

"If you can all please disembark down the emergency chute" asks the Captain

"The chute?" asks the Monsignor

"Sorry, it's standard procedure in an emergency landing" advises the attendant

"Well, the chute … it'll be a first for me" explains the Monsignor

"Me, too" advises Max

"And me" replies Joseph

As all passengers begin to use the emergency chute off the jet, no other major worries have been reported.

All two hundred and fifty passengers have safely been evacuated from the aircraft at Rome International.

Bomb disposal officers are now on board the aircraft.

"I've found it" advises an officer

"Is it safe?" asks the Commanding officer

"It's a device between two cases, this is where the blaze started" explains the officer

"Has it been deactivated?" asks the Commanding officer

"Deactivation, confirmed" replies the officer

"Have you sourced the cause of the fire?" asks the Commanding officer

"A mobile phone battery power bank, may have caused the fire" explains the officer

"OK, we'll leave the Investigators to their job" advises the Commanding officer

Meanwhile, Max, Joseph and the Monsignor are quickly cleared through customs, and jump into a waiting Vatican limousine.

The Monsignor asks the driver for a Vatican update.

"Have there been any further eruptions or earthquakes?" asks the Monsignor

"No, it's all quiet now" replies the driver

Meanwhile, a sudden interruption comes on the limousine radio.

"We interrupt this bulletin to advise that the Vatican has received another sign ... 5777" advises the broadcaster

"It's going full circle" advises Max

"Yes the envelope 5777 the beginning and the end" replies the Monsignor

The limousine speedily negates the streets of Rome, and eventually arrives in Vatican city.

The Monsignor, and his party are ushered into Cardinal Raphael's office in the Palace of the Holy Office.

A few moments later, Cardinal Raphael enters the room. The Monsignor, Max, and Joseph kneel before the Cardinal.

After pondering for a few moments, Cardinal Raphael begins his address.

"The Illuminati have been behind all the cloak and dagger work, but the mystery of 5777 still remains" advises the Cardinal

"Maybe it's God's way of telling us that it's not the end but a new beginning?" answers the Monsignor

"What do you think, Max?" asks Cardinal Raphael

"I can confirm, it may be the answer we've been looking for, and the Shemitah year may be the key" replies Max

"The Shemitah year?" asks the Cardinal

"According to Jewish prophecy, this may well be God's answer, and that a new dawn is about to be born" advises Max

"A new dawn, and a new time?" asks the Cardinal

"Our World of today is full of contempt for God, they think it's safe, and know all the answers" advises Joseph

"I have briefed the Holy Father on the matter" explains Cardinal Raphael

"… and he is about to address the World, shortly" advises the Cardinal

"The prophecy of Fatima is about to happen … there will be more than secrets locked away" advises Joseph

"It's another sign" explains the Monsignor

"God is truly watching over all of us … we must not waste this moment of truth" explains the Monsignor

The Pope is now on his feet, and about to address the World.

Suddenly, a lone white dove flies overhead.

"It's a sign" advises Cardinal Raphael

"A sign from God" answers the Monsignor

The Pontiff begins his address to the crowds in Vatican Square, and to the millions viewing Worldwide …

The Holy Father begins his address in Latin.

"Benedictus Deus in saecula … Blessed Be God Forever" advises the Holy Father

"It is well that God should be forever praised" explains the Pontiff

"God has sent a sign to us all today. This is a new time in the teaching of the World. His glory lives through lives of holiness, generosity, and conformity to the truth. May God's external glory, and blessedness be extended and

experienced in all places, and in all our hearts" advises the Holy Father

"May God be with you, and Bless you in all your lives" explains the Holy Father

The vast crowd in Vatican Square all hail the Holy Father and his address to the World.

The Pontiff leaves the Papal balcony of the Vatican.

Another envelope arrives addressed to Cardinal Raphael at the Palace of the Holy Office in Vatican city. It reads … 5777 power bank … the power and the influence … the year of the Rapture!

"The power bank on the plane" advises the Monsignor

"Is the rapture about to take place, Eminence?" asks the Monsignor

"The time and place is God's to control" replies the Cardinal

"Who knows when that will happen?" answers the Monsignor

A voice from the Heaven's proclaims …

"All who are on the side of truth, hear my voice"

ONE SECOND FROM LIFE …
ONE SECOND FROM DEATH

When a failed assassination attempt takes place, on the fourth of July, American President, James Denver, escapes.

There is also an attempt on The Pope's life in Rome. All World leaders are now in the firing line!

Nuclear Physicist, Andrew Duncan, is found dead after a fall over Niagara Falls, and has nuclear codes and apocalyptic information in his possession.
The Police confirm that Professor Duncan has been murdered.
The American President contacts Cardinal Raphael at the Vatican. The Cardinal appoints Monsignor Kevin O'Flaherty and Professor "Max" Brookstein to investigate on Presidential orders.

What Max and the Monsignor find may lead to a smaller countries detonation of a nuclear device, and it may
signal the apocalyps, and end of World events!

Can Max and the Monsignor find a solution to stop matters getting out of hand?

TO KILL A PRESIDENT

Washington DC … the fourth of July … National

Independence Day.

American President, James Denver is in attendance … but problems arise when he steps out of the Presidential state limousine, nick named The Beast …

TV stations, and News reporters for various channels are in attendance.

A CNN newscaster states …

"Welcome to Washington DC's Independence Parade … we have marching bands with military, and speciality floats … red, white and blue … it's America's birthday!" advises the newscaster

The newscaster continues his open air broadcast to the watching audience of millions across America.

"The Presidential motorcade is due to arrive on the National Mall, any minute" advises the newscaster

Suddenly, the Presidential motorcade arrives accompanied by escorts, front and rear, complete with running Special Agents alongside the President's limousine, The Beast.

FBI and Presidential security guards, all armed, are also sweeping the area for any problems or terrorist activity.

"The President has arrived here at Independence Hall to rapturous applause" advises the newscaster

Television camera's are shooting pictures from every angle.

As the President makes his way out of the beast limousine a single shot rings out.

All the Special Agents and FBI guards advise everyone …

"Take cover" shout several Special Agents

The President is rushed out of sight.
The CNN reporter continues to inform the millions of Americans who are watching the fallout of the parade.
"We interrupt this programme to announce that The President was shot at around midday ... we will update when we have more details" advises the reporter
The Chief of Staff now takes control of the unfolding situation.
"Do you have a word for our fellow Americans?" asks several reporters
"The situation is now in lockdown. I can confirm that the President is OK, but we take this as a warning" advises the Chief of Staff
"We will release more details, when we have them" ends the Chief of Staff
The waiting reporters thank the Chief of Staff but somehow the whole occasion has now gone into meltdown.
"We have a declaration of Independence, and we must protect it ... all who value freedom are on our side" advises the newscaster
Meanwhile, in Rome, The Pontiff is due to give a Papal audience in Vatican Square at 10am. The address is a weekly affair, usually given by the Holy Father on a Wednesday morning ... large crowds are gathered in the Vatican domain.
All the Archbishop's are in attendance, and Monsignor Kevin O'Flaherty is also there accompanying Cardinal Raphael.
The Papal audience usually lasts for about an hour and

a half.

After the Papal mass, The Pontiff will then venture into the waiting crowds in Vatican Square, and he is normally surrounded by security.

"It's a great day for Rome, today, Monsignor" advises Cardinal Raphael

"Indeed it is, your Eminence" replies O'Flaherty

"Are you still in contact with Professor Brookstein?" asks the Cardinal

"Yes, I'm in close contact" replies the Monsignor

The Holy Father concludes the mass, and walks into the crowd, accompanied by lots of security.

The crowd are congregated behind the iron gating system in Vatican Square.

All is well, until … a single shot rings out, narrowly missing the Pontiff.

All the security staff leap into action to protect the Holy Father.

"Did you hear that, Eminence?" asks the Monsignor

"It sounded like a gun shot" explains the Monsignor

"We must hurry to see if His Holiness is alright" replies the Cardinal

"Indeed we must, Eminence" replies the Monsignor

Both the Cardina, and the Monsignor rush into the official residence of the Holy Father, the Apostolic Palace.

The Holy Father is surrounded by doctors, and nurses from Vatican City hospital.

Security is tight, and no one without official Vatican status is allowed into the area.

Cardinal Raphael, one of the Holy Father's most

trusted diplomats rushes over to the Pontiff.

"Are you alright, your Holiness?" asks the Cardinal

"Yes, I am … but it was another close call" replies the Holy Father

"Do you think you should now stop all the audience participation?" asks Cardinal Raphael

"We are servants of God … Our Blessed Lord would have carried on, and I intend to do so too" explains the Holy Father

It's not too long before the World's press get hold of the story, and match it to the fourth of July Presidential attack in the United States.

Back in America, at NASA, a Nuclear Physicist, Andrew Duncan has been found dead, after a presumed fall, over Niagara Falls.

The Police confirm that he was murdered, and found in his possession secret details of nuclear codes and a stark warning to the World!

The Niagara Police Service is a special constabulary maintained by the Niagara Parks Commission in Niagara Falls.

The Chief of Police Commissioner, Bill Leonard contacts NASA.

"We confirm Andrew Duncan, was a Scientist specialising in the production of nuclear energy and weapons for the American government" advises a NASA official

"What was he working on?" asks the Police Commissioner

"Andrew Duncan was linked to top secret security and Atomic nuclear physics … he was a top man and

known to the President" advises the NASA official
"We have found, in his possession, a stark warning … of World importance" advises the Police Commissioner
"Presidential … eyes only" explains the NASA official
"Confirmed" advises the Police Commissioner
"You can scramble the information to the Presidential Chief of Staff" advises the NASA official
"Consider it done" replies the Police Commissioner
In a matter of minutes the sensitive information is dispatched.
The Chief of Staff updates the President in the Oval Office at the Whitehouse.
"I've received valuable information concerning the recent death of Andrew Duncan, the nuclear physicist, Mr President" advises the Chief of Staff
"What does it say, Bob?" asks the President
"It dwells on the end of time … the end of days, and a date in the not too distant future" replies the Chief of Staff
"Doomsday?" asks the President
"Yes, that's what it says, Mr President" advises the Chief of Staff
"Amazing evidence" explains the Chief of Staff
"Do we need a Specialist, to advise us, Bob?" asks the President
"Yes, maybe that would be a good idea" explains the Chief of Staff
"Have you seen the news, Mr President?" asks the Chief of Staff
"Yes, I've seen the failed assassination attempt on the

Pope" replies the President

"I think we'd better contact Cardinal Raphael, we may need his help" asks the President

"I'll ask for a call to be relayed to the Vatican at once" answers the Chief of Staff

A call is made from the Whitehouse directly to Cardinal Raphael's state room in the Holy Office at Vatican City.

A few minutes pass, one of the phones on the President's desk begins to ring.

A Vatican aide answers the phone.

Cardinal Raphael takes the call from the Whitehouse.

"Good afternoon, Cardinal Raphael" advises the President

"Good afternoon, Mr President" answers the Cardinal

"I take it that you are aware of the recent attempt on my life and His Holiness, The Pope?" asks the President

"Yes, I'm fully aware … are you alright Mr President?" asks the Cardinal

"Luckily the bullet missed … we have a diplomatic problem" advises the President

"It also involves the end of time" explains the President

"Are you in need of help and guidance, Mr President?" asks Cardinal Raphael

"Yes, if you can help?" replies the President

"I'll dispatch Monsignor O'Flaherty, at once" advises the Cardinal

"That would be excellent, thank you" replies the President

"We may need Professor Brookstein's assistance too" advises the President

"Don't worry I'll see that they are both dispatched to Washington today" replies the Cardinal

Monsignor O'Flaherty is summoned to Cardinal Raphael's quarters in the Palace of the Holy Office.

The Monsignor is escorted by a personal aide into the Cardinal's quarters.

Cardinal Raphael enters the grand room.

The Monsignor kneels and kisses the Cardinal's ring on entry.

"Please be seated, Monsignor" asks the Cardinal

"I have just spoken with James Denver" informs the Cardinal

"The American President?" replies the Monsignor

"Yes, Monsignor … he has received information with regards to the end of the World prophecy … he has specifically asked for you to swiftly join him at the Whitehouse to assist in investigations" explains Cardinal Raphael

"Yes, I'll go at once" replies the Monsignor

"We've made contact with Professor Brookstein, and she confirms a meeting at Washington International. You have both been given diplomatic clearance, and an escort to the Whitehouse" advises the Cardinal

"What information do we have to go on, Eminence?" asks the Monsignor

The Cardinal continues to brief the Monsignor on his conversations with the American President.

After the meeting, the Monsignor packs several bags and heads to Rome International where he boards an ITA Airways flight directly to Washington DC. The flight takes over ten hours, and as per usual, the Monsignor will change time zones, and no doubt arrive the worse for wear.

Several hours later, the Monsignor arrives at Washington Dulles International Airport.

The Announcer advises the arrival of the Monsignor's flight.

"We announce the arrival of ITA Flight AZ720 from Rome International" advises the airport announcement

The Monsignor makes his way through customs and into the Arrivals waiting area.

The Monsignor spots Professor Brookstein, almost immediately.

"Max" greets the Monsignor

The Professor greets the Monsignor with a kiss on both cheeks.

"Kevin … I'm glad to see you again" advises Max

"Likewise, Max … likewise" replies the Monsignor

"I trust you had a pleasant flight?" asks Max

"Not so bad, but you know, I'm not too keen on long distance flights" replies the Monsignor

"It seems we are needed on Presidential matters, lass" advises the Monsignor

Several Presidential aides arrive at the terminal, and make themselves known to Max, and the Monsignor.

Both flash their Secret Service cards to Max and the Monsignor.

"If you could both please follow us, to the waiting limousine" asks an aide

Max and the Monsignor follow the Secret Service personnel to the waiting blacked out limousine. They jump in and the limo then manoeuvres its way out of Washington Dulles International into a cleared freeway to the Whitehouse.

Max, and the Monsignor arrive at the Whitehouse, where they are met by the Chief of Staff who escorts them through several security checks, then into the Oval Office, in the West Wing. The President is waiting to meet them.

"Good afternoon" advises the President

"Good afternoon, Mr President" respond Max and the Monsignor

"Please, call me James or Jim … whichever takes your fancy, we can be ourselves here until diplomacy calls" explains the President

"Well, what's it all about Jim?" asks the Monsignor

"I take it, Cardinal Raphael has briefed you?" asks the President

"Yes, fully" replies the Monsignor

"Did Cardinal Raphael tell you about the launch codes found in Andrew Duncan's possession?" asks the President

"Yes, and the importance of World peace" responds the Monsignor

"What's your take on it, Professor?" asks the President

"I've been fully briefed too, what is the story regarding the intermediate galactic missiles?" asks Max

"Well, Max, we think the codes found in Andrew Duncan's possession were planted to get our attention by a third World country" explains the President

"So you've ruled out the Russians?" asks the Monsignor

"Do you think Russia is involved?" asks Max

"We're not sure at this stage, Max ... but we believe nuclear weapons maybe" replies the President

"Nuclear?" asks the Monsignor

"If just one of those is launched, it could start World War Three ... Doomsday and the Apocalypse" advises the Monsignor

"So, how can we help?" asks Max

"I'm going to give you both Presidential diplomatic clearance to look into whatever you can find out" replies the President

"We'll look into the nuclear threat, and keep you informed" explains the President

"We've arranged special clearance to all departments, we are at your disposal" advises the President

Max and the Monsignor thank the President.

"Thank you Mr. President" replies the Monsignor

"Please call me James or Jim, Kevin" advises the President

"Thank you James" continues the Monsignor

"Now, the Chief of Staff will escort both of you to our diplomatic suite where you will be our guests throughout the duration" advises the President

The Chief of staff asks Max and the Monsignor to follow him through several safety checks into the diplomatic suite.

"There are about 14,500 nuclear weapons in the World, all are active.

"We have an arsenal of 6,550" informs the Chief of

Staff

"Mass destruction" replies Max

"We are living in a probable war zone" replies the Monsignor

"It's been like that since the Cold War" advises the Chief of Staff

"My God, if the apocalypse comes it may be misread, as a threat, to human kind" explains the Monsignor

"We have Presidential orders to look into that threat" replies Max

"To find an answer, we have to understand the question" advises the Monsignor

"This may be our most important investigation to date, Kevin" advises Max

"The signs are so strong now, and the evidence is so clear, that everyone willing to accept the truth can see, that the end of the World, as we know it, is near" explains the Monsignor

"We are living in perilous times, Kevin" replies Max

"Indeed we are, lass … just how we solve this one … I don't know" advises the Monsignor

Max and the Monsignor arrive at the diplomatic suite. Armed guards patrol the corridors.

"That's not necessary" advises the Monsignor

"It's always necessary in the Whitehouse" replies the Chief of Staff

HANGING BY A THREAD

When a gunman opens fire at a hotel in Dallas, Texas, there are several , and many left dead.
Police advise that a suicide bomber also rammed a car packed with explosives, and ran it into the hotel.
The gunman storms the building.
Terrorists take the blame ... and the American President issues a red alert warning.

The Oval Office at the Whitehouse, Washington DC.
"I want those people stopped, at all costs" advises the President
"They are terrorists, the hotel is now in lockdown" advises the Chief of Staff
"Which hotel was involved, Bob?" asks the President
"It's the Crown Plaza, Dallas Market Center … FBI agents and Security have the place surrounded" explains the Chief of Staff
"Have any hostages been taken?" asks the President
"Affirmative, Mr President … yes they have hostages" advises the Chief of Staff
"That could be tricky … keep me informed, Bob" replies the President
Meanwhile, the Monsignor, and Max are looking into all the leads provided by the President, and his staff.
"The threat is real, Max" advises the Monsignor
"The whole World is on a knife edge" explains the Monsignor
"I agree, Kevin … and this latest situation in Dallas won't help" replies Max
Max advises the Monsignor regarding the hotel bombing.
"Are there many dead, Max?" asks the Monsignor
"Yes, and hostages have been taken" informs Max
"The President will have it under control, we have to look into the probability of nukes, and the end of time" explains Max
Suddenly, a call from the Chief of Staff.
"Hi Monsignor, I take it you've seen the news of the shootings, and bombings in Dallas?" asks the Chief of

Staff

"Yes, I have ... and it really sickens me" replies the Monsignor

"What's happening now, Bob?" asks Max

"We've taken out two terrorists ... one was carrying another sequence of codes for launch sites ... they were terrorists" explains the Chief of Staff

"Have you been able to decipher the codes?" asks the Monsignor

"We are actually looking into that now, we'll update you as soon as we know" replies the Chief of Staff

"Thanks" replies the Monsignor

"The situation is critical, Max ... everything is now hanging by a thread" advises the Monsignor

Meanwhile, in the background, a report is now on television from the Whitehouse Press Secretary ...

"The current situation at the Hotel Crown Plaza in Dallas is in total lockdown ... two terrorists have been taken out by FBI agents, and the last remaining gunman is now being pursued ... all hostages are now free ... I repeat, all hostages are now free" advises the Whitehouse Press Secretary

"Further updates will be forecast when we have them" concludes the Whitehouse Press Secretary

"A terrorist organisation are behind all of this" advises the Monsignor

"Yes, but which country are behind it?" asks Max

"Do we have anything to go on, lass?" asks the Monsignor

"I've looked into the Presidential files, and there are details of several occasions prior to the eye of the prophecy … the Biblical end of the World" replies the Monsignor

"What are the details?" asks Max

"The eye of the prophecy is … Jesus Christ" advises the Monsignor

"Jesus is both the vision seen by a prophet, and is the eye of the prophecy through which a prophet sees" explains the Monsignor

"What else does it say, Max?" asks the Monsignor

"The Torah shines with the news of the Son of God" replies Max

"All things prophesied are about to be fulfilled" explains Max

"Time is of the essence … we may not be able to stop what's about to happen" advises the Monsignor

Suddenly, a news flash appears on all television channels.

"We interrupt this programme to advise that someone has launched a nuclear device into the atmosphere … it's target … the United States … we have launched counter measures to deal with the impending impact" advises the newscaster

"My God, Max … it has started" advises the Monsignor

"What can we do?" asks the Monsignor

"All we can do is hope that the nuclear device is destroyed before it reaches here" replies Max

"All our lives are in the balance, it could be a direct hit … we'll soon know" responds the Monsignor

The Monsignor contacts the President to advise his findings … but he is rebuked as the President has been taken to the nuclear bunker.

"I'm sorry, Monsignor ... due to a pending attack, the President has been dispatched to a secret location away from harm" advises the Chief of Staff

"Tell him, we may have found out what all the information means" advises the Monsignor

"I will send a diplomatic aide, they will escort you, and the Professor out of the area" replies the Chief of Staff

"Thank you" replies Max

"They will be dispatched, shortly" explains the Chief of Staff

Meanwhile, the President is being briefed at a secret location by security staff.

"Nuclear detection, and counter measures have been deployed, Mr President" advises General Newman

"How far away is the missile?" asks the President

"It's not reached American shores yet ... we have the nuclear codes and keys at your disposal" advises the General

"We will only use those, if we have to" advises the President

"Has anyone claimed responsibility?" asks the President

"No one" replies the General

The nuclear and counter measures system is used in an emergency situation.

The capabilities are needed to respond effectively during a nuclear attack, and they are deployed in advance, in hope of stopping the threat.

"The United States faces a threat from an unknown country ... we are under attack" explains the President

"I'll address the nation" advises the President

The Chief of Staff and several armed Secret Service agents escort the President to a diplomatic chamber, where a television crew and cameras have been set up to transmit and record the live announcement, on all channels.

The President is seated behind a large desk and in front of it there is a Presidential seal … THE PRESIDENT OF THE UNITED STATES

A television producer sets the scene, and begins to count down the President to go live on air.
"5, 4, 3, 2, 1 … LIVE" advises the TV producer
The American President begins to deliver his announcement to the nation.
"My fellow Americans, we face our darkest hour since 9/11 … a nuclear device has been deployed, and it is heading for the United States. We have deployed counter measures to destroy the missile, and await clarification. We must put all our trust in God that this terrorist attack, on freedom, will be averted.
May God Bless you all" announces the President
The President leaves the converted room, and asks the Chief of Staff for an update concerning the terrorist attack.
"Has the missile reached our shores yet, Bob?" asks the President
"No, Mr President … it's a long way off … we are hoping that it doesn't have the range" replies the Chief of Staff
"Have counter measures deployed on target?" asks the President

"ETA approx ten minutes" answers the Chief of Staff
While the World waits, the Monsignor, and Max reach the Presidential bunker, and are taken in to the President's quarters.
For a moment, the President reflects on matters with the Monsignor.
"We think we've found the answer, Mr President" advises Max
"We looked meticulously into the paperwork that was sent to us, and it appears that it all comes down to the Eye of the Prophecy" advises the Monsignor
"The Prophecy?" asks the President
"According to the information, all things prophesied, are about to be fulfilled" explains the Monsignor
The Chief of Staff enters the room and confirms ...
"Counter measures have been successful, Mr President ... the nuclear device was destroyed over the Atlantic" advises the Chief of Staff
"We must inform the nation" answers the President
"I'll get back to you Monsignor, you must tell me more of the prophecy" asks the President
The Chief of Staff escorts the President, with several armed Secret Service agents back into the TV recording room, where he begins to address the nation again.
The President is counted in by the Producer ...
A green light advises ... Live transmission.
"My fellow Americans, I can confirm that the nuclear device launched against the United States has been successfully destroyed over the Atlantic ... we are in pursuit of the terrorists behind the attack. We will

advise you further, as and when, we have more details. May God Bless you and keep you all safe. God Bless America!" advises the President

The President leaves the recording room, and goes back into a meeting with the Chief of Staff and Generals, to discuss why this was allowed to take place.

The Monsignor and Max continue to check into the prophecy, and all that it entails.

UNSTOPPABLE

As tensions escalate, a nuclear submarine suddenly disappears in the Atlantic. The American President proclaims, all out war on terrorists, and a search for the submarine begins.
The Monsignor, and Max advise about the prophetic visions of the future. The situation becomes urgent, and critical!
THE WHITEHOUSE, WASHINGTON DC ...
The Chief of Staff briefs the President, in the Oval Office.
"We are unable to make contact with the submarine, Mr President" advises the Chief of Staff
"Does it have nuclear capability, Bob?" asks the President
"Affirmative, but it doesn't have launch codes availability" answers the Chief of Staff
"Without the nuclear codes they are inoperable" replies the President
"I agree, they are rendered harmless" advises the Chief of Staff
"What about breaking the codes?" asks the President
"Can the codes be broken, Bob" adds the President
"That seems, highly unlikely, Mr President" replies the Chief of Staff
"This is an extremely volatile situation, and the

escalation could goad the West into taking very risky … but necessary action" advises the President

"What about localised military action, Bob?" asks the President

"No one has yet accepted liability" replies the Chief of Staff

"We are on urgent standby, and our nuclear force has been dispatched, to the Atlantic, Mr President" explains the Chief of Staff

"What about our other strategic capabilities?" asks the President

"Our star systems are also fully operational" confirms the Chief of Staff

"Keep them on standby, Bob" advises the President

Meanwhile, the Monsignor and Max stumble upon further revelations that may take place.

"We are probably witnessing the signs … of the last days, Max" advises the Monsignor

"The power, and might of the United States may not be the ones who start it off, Kevin" advises Max

"What do you think, Max?" asks the Monsignor

"A smaller country could be behind it all" answers Max

A sudden newsflash on the television …

"We interrupt this programme with regards to the recent disappearance of the nuclear submarine USS Prodigal. It would appear that Iran has accepted responsibility!

"They claim it was violating their International Treaty. We believe this to be a lie" advises the newscaster

The nuclear submarine was on patrol in the Atlantic,

and in International waters" adds the newscaster
"According to our records, Iran has signed the agreement with the United States for the devastation of nuclear weapons" advises the Monsignor
"They are in total violation, Max" adds the Monsignor
"World War Three may be a possibility" answers Max
"The World is full of sin, Max" explains the Monsignor
"Do you think we are living the last days, Kevin?" asks Max
"There has been a degeneration over the last fifty years, and we cannot set dates, but from all the signs, we know the second coming, is at the door, Max" advises the Monsignor
"Max, isn't there a solar eclipse, about to take place?" asks the Monsignor
"Yes, and according to Jewish beliefs, it's a sign of the end of the World" replies Max
"When is it due, Max?" asks the Monsignor
"In about seven days from now" replies Max
"We must advise the President, lass" answers the Monsignor
Back at the Whitehouse, The Chief of Staff is updating the President on the current situation.
"Hurricanes are continuing to wreak havoc in Miami, Mr President … and several earthquakes, on the richter scale 8.2, tremors have also struck Mexico" advises the Chief of Staff
"We are in a grave situation, Bob" replies the President
"Iran have made contact, and claim it was their doing … we have advised them of the International agreement" explains the Chief of Staff

"What's their response?" asks the President
"Absolute silence, Mr President" replies the Chief of Staff
"OK, prepare readiness of the fleet, and await my command" orders the President
"Affirmative, Mr President" answers the Chief of Staff
"We've got a situation here, Bob" advises the President
Meanwhile, Max and the Monsignor arrive at the Oval Room, in the West Wing of the Whitehouse, to update the President.
"Escalation and devastation is all around us" advises the President
"We've looked into a Jewish prophecy" replies the Monsignor
"What did you find?" asks the President
"Over to you, Max" replies the Monsignor
"It seems all the evidence was predicted, a hundred years ago, that all these things that are happening now, would be taking place" advises Max
"A solar eclipse is due to take place in seven days" explains Max
"What does it all mean, Max?" asks the President
"It will be a great sign for the World" explains Max
"This is only the beginning" advises Max
"Is there anything we can do?" asks the President
"The Rabbi predicted the seven Noahide laws must be obeyed, if we ignore this commandment all will suffer" explains Max
The seven Noahide Laws are a set of universal moral laws that were given by God as a covenant with Noah and with all of humanity.

"What does the law say, Max?" asks the Monsignor

"It marks the end of the World ... the one hundred year prophecy predicts the Apocalypse" replies Max

The Chief of Staff returns to the Oval Office with an update regarding the submarine, USS Prodigal.

"We have located the present position of the sub, Mr President" advises the Chief of Staff

"Where is the sub being held, Bob?" asks the President

"Our jet fighters located it in Iranian waters ... warning shots have been fired at our aircraft for violation of their airspace" advises the Chief of Staff

"Put all our fleet on full code RED warning ...and to act only on Presidential orders" advises the President

"I will relay the fleet in readiness, Mr President" advises the Chief of Staff

"The Apocalypse ... Kingdom will rise against Kingdom ... we are on Earth's final days" advises the Monsignor

"What can we do to save the World?" asks the President

"From everything we have checked, it won't be long" advises Max

"How long do we have ... is it years?" asks the President

"No, it won't be years" replies the Monsignor

"It could be in a matter of weeks" advises Max

"The Apocalypse will begin this year ... the end of the World is coming" advises the Monsignor

"Can we do anything to stop it?" asks the President

"All we can confirm, is that it's about to happen" advises the Monsignor

"It's unstoppable, Mr President" advises Max
"A major event is about to take place ... somewhere in the World ... it will trigger doomsday, and the predicted Apocalypse" explains the Monsignor
"Should I make an announcement to the nation?" asks the President
"We think, as all the evidence points to a main event, it maybe significant to address the people now" advises the Monsignor
The President instructs his aides to make the necessary broadcast arrangements from the Oval office. The address to the nation will take place at 2pm with a follow up later in the evening.
"We all thought 2012 was predicted ... and that passed" advises the President
"They got it wrong then, Mr President" replies the Monsignor
"They omitted the time difference, known as the seven years ... that is when the Heavenly wedding is set to begin and that makes it December, but it could be anytime really, Mr President" explains the Monsignor
The Chief of Staff enters the Oval Office to update the President ... and it is grave news!
"Reports have been coming in of a massive earthquake in Los Angeles, Mr President" advises the Chief of Staff
"My God" replies the President
"It is believed there are many casualties, Mr. President" explains the Chief of Staff
"It has begun" advises the Monsignor
"How much time do we have left?" asks the President

"Hours, days, weeks … it's impossible to say" replies the Monsignor

"Have emergency measures been put in place in LA, Bob?" asks the President

"Yes, Mr President … we are on top of the situation" explains the Chief of Staff

"And the nuclear sub?" asks the President

"We await your command" replies the Chief of Staff

"Have we been in contact with regards the sub, Bob?" asks the President

"We have tried to make contact, but all diplomatic channels have failed" explains the Chief of Staff

"Well try again … I'll speak directly to the Iranian President" advises the President

An immediate connection to the Iranian President Ahmed is scrambled to the Whitehouse …

"We have made connection with the Iranian President" advises the Chief of Staff

"OK, Bob, put him through" advises the American President

The President picks up the red scrambled phone in the Oval Office.

"This is American President, James Denver speaking to you from the Whitehouse" advises the President

"Welcome Mr President" greets Iranian President Ahmed

"You appear to be holding one of our vessels, USS Prodigal, which is forbidden under International Law" advises the American President

"Your vessel was in Iranian waters, without any clearance" replies the Iranian President

"We totally refute your claim, and advise that unless you release our vessel immediately, a state of emergency will exist between our countries" explains the American President

TIME SEQUENCE

As the World starts to experience record breaking temperatures, all the talk is of the Apocalypse, and the end of time.
Washington DC is at 45 degrees, London is at 40 degrees, and it is 45 degrees and above in Europe.
The Polar icecaps are beginning to show signs of melting!
Mobile phones and all technology starts to interrupt vital equipment, and communications. To put it mildly, the whole World is in meltdown!
Back in the Whitehouse, American President, James Denver continues to negotiate with the Iranian

President.

Max and the Monsignor are looking into the time sequence of events.

"What have you found out with regards the end of times timeline, Max?" asks the Monsignor

"I've not yet been able to find anything specific, as no date has been given, Kevin" replies Max

"Well, what's your best guess, Max?" asks the Monsignor

"Remember to take into account everything that's happening in the World" explains the Monsignor

"We have at best, several days, Kevin" advises Max

"The whole World is in crisis, economic troubles, uprisings, riots, wars, earthquakes, tidal waves, volcanoes erupting, and now record breaking temperatures, not forgetting the polar icecaps melting" explains Max

"What do you think, Max?" asks the Monsignor

"I believe there is yet another possible huge crisis to come" advises Max

"What is it, Max?" replies the Monsignor

"The catalyst for the governments is another 9/11 (nine eleven) type of terrorist event or a natural disaster … whatever it is, you can bet your bottom dollar, that it's on it's way" explains Max

"We must inform the President" advises the Monsignor

The Monsignor contacts the Chief of Staff who arranges for an immediate meeting with the President in the Oval Office.

The President makes an announcement.

"The World is now uniting under this climate change agenda. We are also supporting the Papacy in Rome" advises the President

The President continues his address.

"A call for World unity, and peace is growing all the time, because of all the troubles in the World, and the Pope is helping with the solution" explains the President

The Chief of Staff updates the President concerning the embargo of USS Prodigal in Iranian waters.

"Due to the current situation with Iran, Mr President, concerning the USS Prodigal ... we are now on a pre-war situation" advises the Chief of Staff

"Continue to await my orders" instructs the President

"We may have to make them" advises the Chief of Staff

The Monsignor begins to update the President.

"If you can hold on that order, Mr President?" asks the Monsignor

"I hope you've come up with something tangible?" asks the President

"According to the Book of Revelation, governments will unite because of all the turmoil in the World. We can no longer blame God for the disasters that are happening in the World" explains the Monsignor

"What have you found out, Kevin?" asks the President

"Is it a sign of the end of times?" adds the President

"Yes, and the time sequence is changing" explains Max

The Chief of Staff pushes the President for an answer concerning the Iranian crisis.

"Advise the Iranians that they need to release USS Prodigal within the next two hours, or they will face a force of such magnitude which has never been seen before on Earth" advises the President

The Chief of Staff nods, and begins to leave the Oval Office.

"Oh, Bob" asks the President

"Yes, Mr President" replies the Chief of Staff

"Make contact with all the other Heads of Government. We need to come together to resolve the impending … end of the World events" orders the President

The President then turns to Max, and the Monsignor.

"Kevin, please contact Cardinal Raphael and request that the Pope also makes contact with regards the solution the World is looking for" asks the President

"Yes, I will, at once, Mr President" replies the Monsignor

The Chief of Staff, suddenly, rushes back into the Oval Office to update the President.

"We are experiencing massive communications at this time … our forces report all weapons are inoperable … the Iranians have agreed to our terms, at the eleventh hour" advises the Chief of Staff

"What's happening, Bob?" asks the President

"The Apocalypse is about to take place" advises the Monsignor

"Have you spoken to Cardinal Raphael?" asks the President

"I have recently spoken to him … I believe the Holy Father is awaiting your call, Mr President" replies the Cardinal

The President calls over the Chief of Staff.

"Patch me through to the Vatican, Bob" asks the President

The Chief of Staff arranges for the call to be made by scramble ...

The President is advised that the Pope is awaiting his call.

The President lifts the receiver and begins to address the Pontiff.

"Good day, your Holiness" advises the President

"Good afternoon, Mr President" replies the Pontiff

"I trust you are aware of the problems facing the World?" asks the President

"Yes, I am ... I believe we need to act fast" answers the Pontiff

"All communications and weapons have been rendered inoperable" advises the President

"The end of time is at hand, and the end of days" replies the Pontiff

The Chief of Staff suddenly interrupts the call.

"Excuse me, Mr President" asks the President

The President puts his hand over the receiver.

"What is it, Bob?" asks the President

"News from NASA" advises the Chief of Staff

"Just one minute, Bob" replies the President

The President begins to talk again to the Holy Father at the Vatican.

"Forgive me, Holy Father, we seem to have a developing situation here, I will call you again shortly" explains the President

The call to the Vatican ends.

"OK, Bob, what have you got?" asks the President

"NASA has advised that a large object in space ... a meteor is on collision course with Earth" explains the Chief of Staff
"Are our Star systems operable?" asks the President
"Affirmative, Mr President ... we only have to lock on to the meteor" advises the Chief of Staff
"OK, Bob ... we are go on that" advises the President
"I'll instruct NASA to commence countdown and ask for the time sequence to be initiated" replies the Chief of Staff
"How far is the meteor from Earth, Bob?" asks the President
"I'm afraid, not far enough ... NASA estimates about 48 hours max" advises the Chief of Staff
"Our weapons are primed, Mr President" advises the Chief of Staff
As the World swelters in the heat, all countries are experiencing climate changes in excess of up to 45 degrees.
News bulletins, broadcast on all channels, are updating concerning the climate changes across the World.
"We interrupt this programme to advise that, in the next few hours, temperatures will plummet to 20 degrees below" advises the newscaster
"The World is in turmoil" advises the Monsignor
"It sounds as if we are in a parallel zone ... neither one thing or the other" explains Max
The President asks the Chief of Staff to reconnect his scrambled call to the Vatican.
Several minutes pass, then suddenly, a red phone on

the President's desk in the Oval Office begins to ring.

"Please accept my apologies for my earlier call, Holy Father" asks the President

The Pontiff accepts the President's apology and then begins to advise him of what he intends to do.

"I have decided to address all the nations of the World" advises the Pontiff

"I, too will do the same, Holy Father" replies the President

"We are in God's hands now" responds the Pontiff

The scrambled call ends.

The meteor's approach towards Earth is becoming more increasingly anxious for all the World's governments.

"We are in an extinction level event situation" advises the President

"I must address the nation, Bob" explains the President

The Chief of Staff arranges for the President to address the nation on all television channels, from the Whitehouse at 6pm.

As the President addresses the nation, Max and the Monsignor are talking with Cardinal Raphael in a video call.

"We have made the President aware of the situation" advises the Monsignor

"He believes that an extinction level event is about to take place" explains Max

Meanwhile, the President is advised by the Chief of Staff that the meteor's approach to Earth has become critical.

"Are we in range of the Star weapons system?" asks the President

"Affirmative, Mr President" advises the Chief of Staff

"We'll only get one shot on the approach … do you want me to contact NASA?" asks the Chief of Staff

"Yes, Bob … do it now" orders the President

NASA is given the Presidential orders by the Chief of Staff.

Several strikes are made on the meteor, but with little or no impact.

The Chief of Staff updates the President.

"NASA advises it's a negative, Mr President" advises the Chief of Staff

"Strikes have been made but on detonation there was little impact on the meteor" explains the Chief of Staff

"We are in God's hands now" advises the Monsignor

"Is there anything else we can do?" asks the President

"This could be the end of the World" replies Max

"But is it?"

DIAGRAMMA VERITAS

(THE DIAGRAM OF TRUTH)

A secret work of scientific facts, written by Galileo is smuggled out of Italy ... and turns up in Holland.

According to legend, the Diagramma della veritas is a fictional book. According to Galileo it contains, secret information. The book has layers and layers of meaning, hidden in the text of the scripture, and if it can be decoded it will reveal everything from the past ... and future events!

When the book is stolen, and turns up in Rome ... Monsignor Kevin O'Flaherty and Professor "Max" Brookstein are placed in charge of finding it ... and deciphering it's meaning!

When a failed assassination attempt on The Pope

takes place, proof is found that it is, in fact, the Monsignor who needs to be eliminated!

To find out the truth, the Monsignor dons several disguises to elude his assailants ... but who is behind it all?
Conspiracy theories, and mystery surrounding events eventually reveal all roads lead to Paris ...and a showdown at The Eiffel Tower!

GALILEO'S SECRET

Brussels, The Grand Place ... a meeting takes place between a selle, and a buyer with regards a priceless book ... Diagramma Veritas ... reportedly lost for centuries, but now turning up on the black market ... the knowledge and facts it contains are thought to be about everything, hidden in the layers of the text, and future events may depend on it's very existence!
At a Bar in The Grand Place, Brussels ...
"Do you have it?" asks the buyer
"Yes, it's in a safe place" advises the seller
"What is the price?" asks the buyer
"You can't put a figure on a priceless relic" answers the seller
"Everything has it's price ... now what is it?" asks the buyer
"Five Million Euro's" replies the seller
"Where, and when?" asks the buyer

"The price does not deter you?" asks the seller
"For something so priceless ... why do you ask about money?" replies the buyer
"OK ... the book is currently in Holland" explains the seller
"I'll need to see it in 48 hours ... can you arrange it by that time?" asks the buyer
"I'll let my contact know ... we'll meet again in 48 hours" answers the seller
"How do I know, you'll honour our deal?" asks the buyer
"You don't ... you'll have to trust me" replies the seller
Both men leave the Grand Place, and arrange to meet at a different location in a couple of days.
The Grand Place is a magnificent central square in the heart of Brussels. It's surrounded by opulent Guild Halls, the city's Town, and the Museum of The City of Brussels.
The second meeting takes place at the Hilton Hotel, which is adjacent to the Grand Place. Both men meet in the opulent bar area.
"Do you have it?" asks the buyer
"I have it" replies the seller
"What about the money?" asks the seller
"It's safe ... payment on receipt" explains the buyer
"OK, we'll do the exchange in Central Station ... on the concourse" advises the seller
"Why not here?" asks the buyer
"Central Station in one hour ... I'll meet you with my associate ... the handover will be done then" explains the seller

An hour later, both men meet in front of the Arrivals and Departures boards in the central hall … a scuffle takes place.
In the scuffle the book is stolen.
Weeks later it turns up in Rome.
Cardinal Raphael summons Monsignor Kevin O'Flaherty to the Palace of the Holy Office in Vatican city.
The Monsignor enters the Cardinal's office, kneels and kisses his ring.
"Good morning, Eminence" greets the Monsignor
"Good day, Monsignor" replies the Cardinal
"Tell me, what do you know of the Diagramma Veritas?" asks the Cardinal
"I know it's Galileo's book of truth, and that it disappeared centuries ago, then turned up in Holland, only for it to disappear again … never to be seen" answers the Monsignor
"What if I was to tell you that it has suddenly turned up, here in Rome?" asks the Cardinal
"When exactly, your Eminence" asks the Monsignor
"Just a few days ago" explains the Cardinal
"How?" asks the Monsignor
"Our contacts advise of a secret meeting in Brussels … and the book being stolen, then eventually turning up here in Rome" explains Cardinal Raphael
"How extraordinary" replies the Monsignor
"Are you aware of it's importance, Monsignor?" asks the Cardinal
"I know of it's layers of information in the text, that's all I know" replies the Monsignor

"Why?" asks the Monsignor

"We need you and the Professor to track it down, and advise if it can be decoded" explains the Cardinal

"Decoded?" asks the Monsignor

"Do you have any leads, Eminence?" asks the Monsignor

"We'll put you in touch with our contacts, Monsignor … you may need help to decipher the code" advises the Cardinal

"We'd already spoken to Professor Kellerman in Oxford" explains the Cardinal

"Excellent, I'll contact Max … I mean Professor Brookstein at once … I'll keep you informed concerning our investigation, Eminence" replies the Monsignor

"Give Max my regards" laughs the Cardinal

The Monsignor leaves the Cardinals meeting room at the Palace of the Holy Office. He immediately contacts Professor Brookstein on his mobile phone.

The number rings out, then suddenly a voice answers.

"Hello, Kevin" answers Max

"How did you know it was me?" asks the Monsignor

"Women's intuition, I guess" laughs Max

"Lovely to hear from you, Kevin" replies Max

"You too, Max" replies the Monsignor

The Monsignor begins to brief Max about the Diagram of Truth.

"Yes, I'm aware of it's existence" explains Max

"Cardinal Raphael has already contacted Robert, in Oxford, for help with regards to deciphering the code" advises the Monsignor

"That's an excellent move, Kevin" answers Max

"I wouldn't know where to begin" explains Max

"Nor would I, Max ... I've studied Latin but the context of the Diagramma Veritas is complicated ... we need professional help, and Robert is the man to do it" replies the Monsignor

"I agree, Kevin" answers Max

"When can you get here?" asks the Monsignor

"I can be on the next plane from John F Kennedy, New York to Rome" explains Max

"OK, Max ... I'll make a special envoy request, on behalf of the Vatican, on your arrival, and I will personally meet you at Rome International" advises the Monsignor

"What about, Professor Kellerman?" asks Max

"Robert is due to arrive at Rome International later today" explains the Monsignor

"OK, I'll let you know my ETA, Kevin" advises Max

"QED" answers the Monsignor

"What does QED mean, Kevin?" asks Max

"It's Latin for Quoderat demonstrandum ... and it literally means to be shown, or as we Irish would say ... quite easily done" explains the Monsignor

Professor Brookstein takes a flight from John F Kennedy airport, New York.

The Monsignor first arranges to meet Professor Robert Kellerman at Ciampino airport.

This is the secondary International airport in Rome, and it is one of the busiest in Italy. It handles over six million passengers a year.

Robert is met by the Monsignor in the Arrivals lounge.

"Welcome, my dear friend ... Robert, how are you?" asks the Monsignor

"I'm glad to be here, Kevin ... and to be asked by Cardinal Raphael to decipher the Diagramma Veritas" replies Robert

The Professor and the Monsignor are met by a waiting Vatican limousine, and they have been given special clearance, and an escort to Vatican city.

Robert and the Monsignor jump into the vehicle, and continue their conversation.

"Well, we've actually yet to receive the book, but our contacts are on to it, we're surely to be briefed about that, later, Robert" advises the Monsignor

"Tell me, Kevin, have you been practising your golf?" asks Robert

"Oh, yes ... the Vatican boasts one of the most spectacular courses" replies the Monsignor

The black limousine weaves in and out of the heavy traffic, and eventually arrives at Vatican City.

Robert and the Monsignor get out of the limousine, and proceed on foot, to the Palace of the Holy Office, where Cardinal Raphael is awaiting their arrival.

Robert and the Monsignor are met by a Papal aide in the opulent surroundings of the Cardinal's quarters.

"The Cardinal is awaiting your attendance" advises the Aide

The Monsignor enters ... kneels and kisses the Cardinal's ring.

Robert follows, into yet another opulently furnished room, with ambient surroundings.

"Good afternoon, Eminence" advises the Monsignor

"Good afternoon, Monsignor … welcome Professor Kellerman" replies Cardinal Raphael
Both men shake hands, as if they have known each other years.
"Please call me Robert" greets the Professor
"Thank you, I will" replies the Cardinal
"We don't stand on ceremony here, Robert … don't you agree Kevin?" asks the Cardinal
"Wholeheartedly" replies the Monsignor
"I take it, the Monsignor, has briefed you with regards events concerning the book?" asks the Cardinal
"Yes, he has, Eminence … and very eloquently too" replies Robert
"We have managed to locate the book's whereabouts through various contacts in the Vatican … are you aware of it's scientific importance in today's World, Robert?" asks the Cardinal
"I have to admit, it's a book I'm not really familiar with … deciphering it's texts may prove to be far more trickier, than I'd hoped" replies Robert
A sudden knock on the door, followed by a Papal Aide entering the room.
"I'm sorry to disturb you, Eminence" advises the Aide
"What is it Antonio?" asks the Cardinal
"A call for the Monsignor, Eminence … from Professor Brookstein" explains the Aide
"I think the Professor may have arrived at Rome International" advises the Monsignor
"Very well … I will give you both leave to meet her" advises the Cardinal
"Perhaps we could all meet later, and then decide on

the line of approach we will take concerning the book" explains the Cardinal

"Indeed, Eminence ... we will keep you updated" replies the Monsignor

The Monsignor kneels and kisses the Cardinal's ring.

Robert and the Monsignor leave the Palace of the Holy Office, and proceed by Vatican limousine to Fiumicino Rome International Airport.

Robert and the Monsignor await the arrival of Flight 714 from John F Kennedy, New York ... the airport announcer advises suddenly ...

"Flight 714 from John F Kennedy, New York ... has been delayed" advises the announcer

Robert and the Monsignor are both not surprised by the announcement.

Then, suddenly, another announcement ...

"Flight 714 from New York is now due to arrive at Rome International at 17.15pm" advises the announcer

"That's in an hours time, Robert!" advises the Monsignor

"What about some refreshment?" asks Robert

"I thought you'd never ask" quips the Monsignor

Robert and the Monsignor head for the Arrivals Bar

"What can I get you?" asks the Barman

"I'll have a brandy" replies Robert

"What'll it be Kevin?" asks Robert

"Do you have Guinness?" asks the Monsignor

"Coming right up" advises the Barman

"We've arranged for special clearance for Max" advises the Monsignor

The drinks arrive in record time.

An hour later, Flight 714 taxies on to the runway and arrives, an hour late!

Professor Brookstein is ushered through the special clearance channels, and meets the Monsignor and Robert in the "special" arrivals area.

She kisses both men, on both cheeks.

"Welcome back, to Rome" greets the Monsignor

"Hello to you too … nice to see you again, Robert" advises Max

"I've been reading all the information you sent me, with regards to Galileo's secret … it's fascinating" explains Max

"Our contacts in Vatican city have assured us, it's the real thing" advises the Monsignor

"What about it's content?" asks Max

"Over to you, Robert" replies the Monsignor

Robert begins his explanation and updates Max.

"Well, I've seen a manuscript, but the real thing, will be very different, and very difficult to translate" advises Robert

"Why?" asks Max

"It's codes and texts are complex … Galileo used an unusual type of writing in the book … even the paper it's written on may hold various unknown secrets" explains Robert

"We have all the modern day technology at our disposal, but it may take some time to decipher the whole book" advises Robert

"That's why it's been lost for centuries" advises the Monsignor

"Yes, that's why" replies Robert

"The Cardinal thinks it's something to do with the Papacy, and the Vatican Council … the secrets in the book could therefore be, very damaging" explains Robert

Max, Robert, and the Monsignor get into the waiting black limousine which whisks them to Vatican City.

The limousine speeds towards the Vatican, and is met by lots of Police and Security. The vehicle has diplomatic plates, and Vatican approval. It is immediately escorted into the complex of buildings.

The Monsignor, Max and Robert head for the offices of the Holy See.

A Papal Aide asks the Monsignor to switch on the television for the latest news.

"We interrupt this bulletin to bring you news of a failed assassination attempt on His Holiness The Pope" advises the newscaster

"My God, the Holy Father … an assassination attempt" replies the Monsignor

"We have several, conflicting reports" explains the newscaster

"We will advise more details, when we get them" ends the newscaster

Cardinal Raphael summons the Monsignor to his meeting rooms at the Palace of the Holy Office.

The Monsignor enters Cardinal Raphael's room where he is greeted on arrival.

The Monsignor kneels and kisses the Cardinal's ring.

"Are you aware of the attempt on the Holy Father's life?" asks the Cardinal

"I am, Eminence … is he alright?" asks the Monsignor
"He is, Monsignor" replies the Cardinal
"We have found proof, through Vatican security channels, that it is, in fact, your life that's at risk" explains the Cardinal
"My life?" replies the Monsignor
"I didn't know I was so important … I'm just a humble Monsignor" answers O'Flaherty
"You've become hot property, Monsignor" advises Cardinal Raphael
"We've placed a Vatican guard, outside your quarters" advises the Cardinal
"But, it's preposterous, Eminence" replies the Monsignor
"Nevertheless, you are important to the Holy See, and the Holy Father has instructed that we have to check into everything" explains the Cardinal
"You will be notified once we've looked into the matter" advises the Cardinal
"I, totally understand, Eminence" advises the Monsignor

ROMAN INTUITION

After an assassination attempt on the Holy Father

in Rome, evidence is found that it is, in fact, the Monsignor who needs to be eliminated.

While the Vatican checks into several leads of inquiry … The Monsignor dons several disguises to elude his pursuers … but in doing so, finds himself, and both Professor's in the firing line again!

The Monsignor's quarters in the Holy See.

"Whatever are you doing, Kevin?" asks Professor Kellerman

"Oh, it's an old dotage of mine … if you can't get out of Vatican city as yourself … become someone else" replies the Monsignor

"Someone else?" asks Robert

The Monsignor suddenly turns towards Robert.

"Well, Robert … how do I look?" asks the Monsignor

"A postman" replies Robert

"I'm not looking over the top am I, Robert?" asks the Monsignor

"Well, maybe a little different, Kevin" answers Robert

"I don't think I'd be able to recognise you" advises Robert

"Excellent … that's what illusion is all about" replies the Monsignor

"Just one question?" asks Robert

"How do you intend to get out of your Quarters … remember a Papal guard has been posted outside your door" advises Robert

"Good question, Robert" replies the Monsignor

"There's another way out of here" advises the Monsignor

"The window?" asks Robert

"No, another connecting door into the Mother Superior's Quarters" explains the Monsignor
"Won't they recognise you, Kevin?" asks Robert
"Yes, of course they will … they are all part of my plan" answers the Monsignor
"What next?" asks Robert
"Maybe a disguise as a nun?" advises Robert
"Don't tempt me, Robert" replies the Monsignor
The Monsignor suddenly leaves his Quarters disguised as a postman, and begins to make his way, out of Vatican city.
"I'll meet you both on the outside, near the left fountain … in 15 minutes" advises the Monsignor
"We'll be there, Monsignor" advises Robert
"Drop the title, Robert … see you there in 15 minutes" replies the Monsignor
Max and Robert rendezvous with the Monsignor at one of the Vatican fountains.
"Why all the cloak and dagger stuff, Kevin?" asks Max
"The Vatican contacts now have the book in their possession … I've arranged to meet someone connected with it's origins here in Rome" advises the Monsignor
The Monsignor's mobile phone begins to ring …
"It's Cardinal Raphael" advises the Monsignor
"I'll have to take the call" explains the Monsignor
The Cardinal begins to explain and update the Monsignor.
"We've found the book, Monsignor … ask Professor Kellerman to report back to my office, and the deciphering can begin" instructs the Cardinal

"How did you know I was out of my office, Eminence?" asks the Monsignor

"Your disguise as a postman was becoming very amusing, but I fully understand your need to investigate, Monsignor" replies the Cardinal

"I'm actually on my way with Max to meet someone who can fully analyse the text, and meaning of the book, here in Rome" advises the Monsignor

"They, and the information they possess will assist us in finding out just what the meaning is of Galileo's secret" explains the Monsignor

"Yes, of course, use your Roman instinct and intuition, wisely, Monsignor" advises the Cardinal

" … and your Irish charm and knowledge" adds the Cardinal

"Yes, thank you … I will, Eminence" replies the Monsignor

Suddenly, there is movement close to the fountain.

"We have to go, Kevin" advises Max

"We are being pursued, Eminence … we must leave" advises the Monsignor

The call ends. Max and the Monsignor make their way out of the Vatican concourse.

Two, rather surly looking characters, follow and are in pursuit.

Max and the Monsignor, still disguised as a postman, are now on the streets close to Vatican city

"Are they Mafia or Illuminati?" asks Max

"It's hard to tell, Max" replies the Monsignor

"Quick, hop on board a tour bus … we'll jump off at the Colosseum" advises the Monsignor

Max and the Monsignor run towards the waiting City Sight Seeing Roma, open topped double decker bus. Lots of tourists are also boarding.

Hot in pursuit are the unknown assailants.

The commentary begins in English.

"Welcome aboard your prestige Roma Sight Seeing Tour … we will point out all the places of interest, along the route" advises the taped announcement

The announcements are then broadcast in several languages to all the other tourists on board the bus.

The open top tour commences, and the bus makes several, hop on hop off stops, along the route.

"OK, next stop is ours" advises the Monsignor

"You've been rumbled" replies Max

"Even the Papal guards, and our own contacts, may be seconded to rival organisations" explains the Monsignor

"It's me they are after, Max" advises the Monsignor

"I've got an idea" replies the Monsignor

The Monsignor takes out his mobile and phones one of the Papal Aides.

He asks for the Aide to meet him, in an hour, at the Colosseum.

"Are our followers still behind, Max?" asks the Monsignor

"Yes, just a few seats behind us" replies Max

"OK … this is the plan" advises the Monsignor

The open topped bus continues it's journey and eventually arrives at the Colosseum in central Rome.

The Monsignor and Max make a scramble to get off the bus and enter the Colosseum, pursued by their followers.

A swap takes place. The Monsignor's role as a postman is taken over by a Papal Aide.

"OK, Max … if you go with Peter, continue the illusion" advises the Monsignor

"I'll meet you, at the next rendezvous" explains the Monsignor

"OK, Kevin, see you soon" replies Max

Peter and Max board the next tour bus. Peter is now in place as another postman. The Monsignor changes back into his robes, which were concealed in his postman's sack.

The plan has worked! The followers are now back on the tour bus, leaving the Monsignor free to make his rendezvous, with his contact.

The Monsignor takes out his mobile phone, and calls the contact.

"Jean Claude we'll meet as arranged at the Colosseum RistoBar on via di San Giovanni … do you know it?" asks the Monsignor

"Yes, I know it" advises Jean Claude

"OK, 20 minutes" advises the Monsignor

The RistoBar is a hive of hustle and bustle, staff are very attentive with many tables to serve. Lots of tourists eat there.

"What can I get you, Father?" asks a Waiter

"I'll have a strong black coffee, please" advises the Monsignor

"Make that two" says another voice

A typical good looking Italian man, dressed in a cream flannel suit with open necked white shirt, sits at the table with the Monsignor

"Did you manage to shake off your followers?" asks Jean Claude

Yes, well and truly ... were you followed? asks the Monsignor

"No, I made sure, no one followed me" replies Jean Claude

"Welcome, Jean Claude" greets the Monsignor

"I take it this is not one of your usual places, for meetings?" asks Jean Claude

"You should see me, when I really go to town" quips the Monsignor

The Monsignor's phone starts to ring.

It's Professor Robert Kellerman with an update.

"Hello Robert, how are you doing with the codes and deciphering of the text?" asks the Monsignor

"I've managed to break down some of the text ... the wording and intricate information used by Galileo is tricky ... but some of it points to a meeting of minds ... in Paris" replies Robert

"Paris?" asks the Monsignor

"Precisely, and it does implicate the Vatican ... but the rest of the text, including the ghostly paper, is transparent ... meaning it could eventually lead us to the answer of creation, and end of time events" explains Robert

"Fascinating, absolutely fascinating" replies the Monsignor

"End of time events?" asks the Monsignor

"OK, continue the good work, Robert ... has Peter and Max returned to see you?" replies the Monsignor

"They are just entering my office, Kevin" advises Robert

"Ask them if they managed to escape their pursuers?" asks the Monsignor

"Affirmative, Kevin ... mission accomplished" replies Robert

"OK, I'll see you in an hour ... we must plan our next move, and I'll discuss it with Jean Claude" advises the Monsignor

The call between Robert and the Monsignor ends.

The Monsignor continues his conversation with Jean Claude.

"A meeting of minds in Paris ... does that mean anything to you, Jean Claude?" asks the Monsignor

"I've heard on the grapevine, that powerful minds, are due to meet in Paris ... but that is all I know" advises Jean Claude

"Do you know, where and when?" asks the Monsignor

"Possibly at the Louvre Pyramid" explains Jean Claude

"That's a famous landmark ... why would they want to draw attention to themselves, in broad daylight?" asks the Monsignor

"We are assuming that it will be a daylight meeting ... when it could easily be at night" replies Jean Claude

"What about a gala or grand event ... something that would detract the eye of any wishful observer?" asks the Monsignor

"Yes, it's possible" replies Jean Claude

The Monsignor begins to check into the itinerary of the Pyramid on his phone.

"Here's something" advises the Monsignor

"In a few days time ... a black tie event" explains the Monsignor

"That's it" replies Jean Claude

"Time for another disguise, Monsignor?" asks Jean Claude

"Exactly ... we'll liaise with Robert ... let's see what else he can find out in the intricacies of the book" explains the Monsignor

Conspiracy theories are evident, but is a high ranking Vatican official the brain behind it all?

What the Monsignor finds, may turn into more than a theory!

In fact, the whole World's survival, may depend on it!

DIVINE EXPECTATIONS

In the finale, all roads lead to the Louvre Pyramid in Paris.
Robert Kellerman's theory confirms Galileo's secret text, was in fact, real, and conspiracy theories lead the Monsignor and Max right into a trap.
A thrilling finale at the Eiffel Tower!
The Monsignor returns to Vatican city after his meeting with Jean Claude.
He joins Professor Robert Kellerman, and is briefed, on the latest findings concerning the text.
"I've virtually broken down the text, and transposition of Galileo's secret" advises Robert
"What have you found, Robert?" asks the Monsignor
"It was, in fact, a divine recollection, through the centuries. It confirms the secret meetings, taking place, all over the World" explains Robert
"What else does it reveal?" asks the Monsignor
"It seals the World's fate, with a possible dramatic conclusion" advises Robert

"Are the Illuminati involved?" asks the Monsignor

"It's hard to say, Kevin … the text does not specify who the parties are, it only gives the necessary confirmation details, of a time line of events" explains Robert

"Where's Max?" asks the Monsignor

"I'm here, Kevin … I've been assisting Robert, with the text" advises Max

"We must see Cardinal Raphael, to advise him of our findings" advises Robert

"I agree … I'll make arrangements to see him at once" replies the Monsignor

"Where to, next?" asks Max

"Paris, is the indication" replies Robert

"The Louvre Pyramid, to be precise" explains Robert

Robert, Max and the Monsignor initiate a meeting with Cardinal Raphael.

They enter the Palace of the Holy Office, where they are met by a Papal Aide.

Cardinal Raphael suddenly enters the ornate room, and welcomes Max, Robert and the Monsignor.

"The Holy Father has asked me to convey his thanks to you all, for all the hard work your doing on behalf of the Holy See" advises the Cardinal

"Is the Holy Father alright, Eminence, after his scare?" asks the Monsignor

"Yes, Monsignor, the Holy Father is in good shape … but he is very concerned about you" advises the Cardinal

"I'm OK, Eminence … I've donned a few disguises, in order to eradicate myself of the oncoming problems" replies the Monsignor

Robert begins to update Cardinal Raphael.

"We've discovered a break through in Paris" advises Robert

"Where exactly, Professor?" asks the Cardinal

"The Galileo text, confined in the book, points to a meeting at the Louvre … it mentions a glass structure. I take it to mean the Louvre Pyramid, and I have managed to decipher the date" advises Robert

"When?" asks the Cardinal

"It is to take place, in the next few days" explains Robert

"Do you think it's a coincidence, that everything seems to be falling to place?" asks Cardinal Raphael

"Yes, I do … it's almost too good to be true, Eminence" advises the Monsignor

"Your all seconded to Paris" advises the Cardinal

"Your meeting awaits … if you could keep me briefed at all times" adds the Cardinal

"We will, Eminence" replies the Monsignor

The Monsignor kneels and kisses the Cardinal's ring.

Max, Robert and the Monsignor leave the meeting, and walk out of the Palace of the Holy Office.

Arrangements have been made by the Holy See for Max, Robert and the Monsignor to take the plane from Rome International to Paris.

Early arrival, Paris. Max, Robert and the Monsignor arrange an evening meeting with a contact.

Jean Claude contacts the Monsignor. He too has just arrived in Paris.

The Monsignor's mobile phone begins to ring.

"The Louvre Pyramid, in one hour" advises the voice

"We'll be there, Jean Claude" replies the Monsignor

The Louvre Pyramid's design was controversial when it was first proposed, but those days are long ago. Now the all glass Pyramid is a permanent fixture on the Parisian landscape. It is looked upon as a design of beauty, and it works majestically in sharp contrast to the buildings surrounding it.

All three arrive at the Louvre Pyramid, where Jean Claude is waiting.

The Monsignor greets Jean Claude, and he introduces Max and Robert

Jean Claude begins to update the Monsignor.

"What have you found out, Jean Claude?" asks the Monsignor

"There's a meeting scheduled for tomorrow" advises Jean Claude

"… and it's purpose?" asks the Monsignor

"I can't find out anything about it … the meeting is shrouded in secrecy" explains Jean Claude

"What's the plan?" asks Max

"I've managed to get you, black market tickets, for the event" advises Jean Claude

"Will anyone suspect?" asks Robert

"No one" replies Jean Claude

"We need to overthrow the controlling party, and bring them to justice" advises the Monsignor

"Have you a plan?" asks Max

"I've arranged for a little diversion, for later" replies Jean Claude

"How do you want to play it, Monsignor?" asks Jean

Claude

"It's vital that we draw them out, into the open" replies the Monsignor

"Cast out the devil, so to speak" explains the Monsignor

"What about the Police?" asks Robert

"We'll ask for a presence at the Pyramid ... the continuation of the World may rely upon what's about to take place" answers the Monsignor

"Do you have the codes?" asks Jean Claude

"Codes?" asks Max

"Yes ... it was encrypted with the book's text, but Galileo's secret is fully encrypted on all messages" advises Robert

"And they are?" asks Jean Claude

"That something is about to take place, here and now" advises Robert

"What, exactly?" asks Jean Claude

"A cycle of events, a sequence of facts, and figures, that will merge into one ... the very essence of time itself" explains Robert

"What's the mission of the secret organisation?" asks the Monsignor

"If I am right ... something will occur when all the pieces are in place" advises Robert

"Like a jigsaw" replies Max

"Exactly ... each piece will fit into it's place ... but this isn't a game" advises Robert

"We're playing, for our very existence" explains Robert

"Is the Vatican implicated?" asks the Monsignor

"The encrypted messages in the text of the book, only gave reference to the Vatican state, and the Pope ... I couldn't find any trace of anything else" explains Robert

Max, Robert, and the Monsignor agree to meet Jean Claude the next day.

"OK, Jean Claude ... tomorrow evening at 8pm ... I guess all will be revealed then" advises the Monsignor

Max, Robert and the Monsignor make their way, to a nearby Parisian cafe.

The Monsignor places the order with the waiter. Max and Robert are seated outside the cafe facing the Louvre Pyramid.

"If, as I expect, all the pieces will come together" advises Robert

"I've briefed, the Police Commissioner" advises the Monsignor

"He is at our disposal" explains the Monsignor

Next day, the meeting takes place at the Louvre Pyramid, as planned.

The Monsignor dons a black evening suit, and a dark wig, to hide his identity.

Max, Rober, and Jean Claude are also attending the exclusive event.

Inside the Louvre Pyramid the meeting takes place in a sealed off area.

"Welcome all to the Louvre Pyramid ... and our meeting of minds" greets the master speaker

"We have many distinguished guests tonight ... but first down to business" advises the speaker

"As you maybe aware, we meet as a force of global

expertise, and it is our intention to secure full control of the World's assets" explains the speaker

"Call us high ranking officials of diplomacy" advises the speaker

"Diplomacy in what?" asks a voice

"and you are?" replies the speaker

"James Whitney … Bank of Ireland" replies the voice

It is in fact, the Monsignor in disguise.

The Chairman whispers to an Aide.

"I think we've been rumbled … time to leave" advises the Chairman

The Monsignor, heavily disguised, leaves, followed by several aides.

"Not very tactful, Monsignor" advises Jean Claude

"I wanted to get a reaction" explains the Monsignor

"Well, you certainly got one" replies Max

"They have got Galileo's Book of Secrets" advises Robert

"That's why" explains the Monsignor

"Follow them" shouts a Police Officer

"Where to next, Monsignor?" asks Jean Claude

"Restaurant 58, Eiffel Tower" advises the Monsignor

"Why?" asks Max

"All will be revealed, Max … all will be revealed" replies the Monsignor

"But the restaurant has been closed, for some time now" advises Jean Claude

"Exactly, it is to the public … but it will give us some cover, and time to draw them out" explains the Monsignor

"How do you know all of this, Kevin?" asks Robert

"Trust me, that's where they are going" replies the Monsignor

"If I'm right, the top man, will be there" explains the Monsignor

"How?" asks Max

"We hold the balance of power, Max" replies the Monsignor

After an energetic race to the Eiffel Tower … the Monsignor changes back into his robes.

Max, Robert, and Jean Claude lie in wait at the now defunct restaurant.

As predicted, The Chairman enters with his aides.

Robert, Max and Jean Claude jump out of the shadows. The Monsignor is now, face to face, with the Chairman.

"Well, are you Illuminati or what?" asks the Monsignor

"We are … who we are … there's no need for names" replies the Chairman

"You are Illuminati" replies the Monsignor

"What are your intentions?" asks Robert

"We aim to take control of the World's activities" replies the Chairman

"You'll never do it" answers Max

"Now, where is the book?" asks the Chairman

"You didn't think we'd bring the real thing with us did you?" replies the Monsignor

"Where is it?" asks Jean Claude

"It's back in Vatican city" explains Robert

"The book is fake" advises the Monsignor

"There are no secrets … it's worthless" advises Robert

"You've been had" explains Max
"Your try at World dominance is over, my friend" advises the Monsignor
"We still have you" advises the Chairman
"Hardly ... you see the Eiffel Tower is surrounded by armed Police ... your time is up" explains the Monsignor
Suddenly, the Police Commissaire enters and takes control of the situation.
"You'll never prove it ... I'll be out in a week" replies the Chairman
"Others will follow" explains the Chairman
"As long we we have the book, the World is safe" advises the Monsignor
The Police take them all into custody.
Max, Robert and the Monsignor return to Vatican city.
Jean Claude is made a Freeman of France for all his bravery, by the French President.
Cardinal Raphael summons the Monsignor to his study at the Palace of the Holy Office.
"On behalf of the Holy Father and World Governments I offer our sincere thanks" advises the Cardinal
"Is the book safe, Eminence?" asks the Monsignor
"No one knows the whereabouts of the book ... it seems after you left, the real Galileo's secrets left Vatican city" explains the Cardinal
"Do we know where?" asks the Monsignor
"No" responds the Cardinal
Maybe it will be lost for centuries again?
We all live in it's shadow and the World must wait again until those secrets are eventually revealed.

THE VATICAN MONSIGNOR

IL MONSIGNORE VATICANO

THE SAVIOUR'S COMING

THY WILL BE DONE

THE MAGDALENE MYSTERY

THE POWER AND THE GLORY

SIGNS FROM HEAVEN

*ONE SECOND FROM LIFE …
ONE SECOND FROM DEATH*

DIAGRAMMA VERITAS (THE DIAGRAM OF TRUTH)

Copyright - Gerry Cullen 2024

THE MAIN CHARACTERS

Introducing … Monsignor Kevin O'Flaherty.

The Monsignor is an unorthodox Irish Roman Catholic Priest, based at the Holy See in the Vatican, and Head of Investigations. He has a nose for solving the unknown.

The Monsignor is six feet tall, has brown hair and green eyes. He is in his mid forties, very astute, and is of a proud Irish background. He was ordained in Dublin, and possesses a sharp wit and sense of humour.A typical Irishman, with a lilting Dublin accent.

Favourite Quotes … It's one thing to have knowledge but another thing to have wisdom. They see but they lack vision. How well can you know anyone?

The Monsignor has a keen interest in golf, all things Irish and loves the classics.

The Monsignor reports directly to Cardinal Raphael

and His Holiness the Pope, Supreme Pontiff of Rome.

THE MAIN CHARACTERS

Introducing … Monsignor Kevin O'Flaherty.

The Monsignor is an unorthodox Irish Roman Catholic Priest, based at the Holy See in the Vatican, and Head of Investigations. He has a nose for solving the unknown.

The Monsignor is six feet tall, has brown hair and green eyes. He is in his mid forties, very astute, and is of a proud Irish background. He was ordained in Dublin, and possesses a sharp wit and sense of humour. A typical Irishman, with a lilting Dublin accent.

Favourite Quotes … It's one thing to have knowledge but another thing to have wisdom. They see but they lack vision. How well can you know anyone?

The Monsignor has a keen interest in golf, all things Irish and loves the classics.

The Monsignor reports directly to Cardinal Raphael

and His Holiness the Pope, Supreme Pontiff of Rome.

Cardinal Raphael … is a devout member of the College of Cardinals at the Palace of the Holy Office in the Vatican. He is astute and wise, a leader. He is a confidante of the Holy Father.

Cardinal Raphael ensures that the Monsignor is effective as Head of Investigations, and frequently sends him into unknown territory, on various assignments to find explanations.

Professor "Max" Brookstein is about five foot eight, slim build, has jet black long hair, blue eyes, in her mid thirties and attractive. She always dresses very smart in her designer suits and attire. You wouldn't think she was a Professor at all. She has a good sence of humour and has a flair for the extraordinary!

The Professor is based in New York city, and part of the Monsignor's Investigations unit. Both have a mutual respect for each other and work well together.

The Professor reports to Cardinal Raphael at the Vatican.

Professor Robert Kellerman is based in Oxford. He is renowned, and works with the Monsignor on various investigations. The Professor is an Oxford academic, he is five foot ten, has blue eyes, brown hair and has a professional look about him.

AUTHOR'S THANKS

Thank you for purchasing a copy of THE VATICAN MONSIGNOR - THE SAVIOUR'S COMING.

I hope you find it heart warming, and that you take to the characters as I have.

I don't feel as if they are my babies but they all drive the story, and give it momentum!

I have to tell you that when I begin to write any story, I really have no idea where I am going!

Sometimes I may hear something, read something or see something that inspires me, and basically that's it. Then I write the precis of the story and tackle the manuscript. It's as simple as that! Everything is hand written!

But as always, I believe that someone else writes the story. It cannot really be me! Yet in essence I am the author!

Please enjoy!!!

THE VATICAN MONSIGNOR

FAVOURITE QUOTES

IT'S ONE THING TO HAVE KNOWLEDGE, AND ANOTHER THING TO HAVE WISDOM

I SEEK NOT TO KNOW ALL THE ANSWERS BUT TO UNDERSTAND THE QUESTIONS

THEY SEE BUT THEY LACK VISION

HOW WELL CAN YOU KNOW ANYONE?

MY CONTINUING REAL COMA STORY

It is now 6 years since I had my life saving open heart surgery at Leeds General Infirmary.

I have written 109 TV series to date, and had 4 books published. I plan to publish another 3 books this year, 2024!

Time is of the essence!

My very real and true story continues today!

Read my true story

BETWEEN WORLDS: MY TRUE COMA STORY

INSPIRATION

The Vatican Monsignor was developed in January 2019, and the inspiration to write an on going series.

This is what happened ...

A religious calendar fell to the ground in our dining room, and it landed face down with a prayer on the back of it. Up to that point I had no idea how I was going to write any story.

The prayer inspired me to write THE SAVIOUR'S COMING. I had to create charcters to obviously look into investigations and unexplained phenomenon.

All of the stories are based on real events. I call them fiction based on fact! All of my books are!

A second series of Investigations will be adapted into another book in March 2025.

Happy reading

FOLLOW ME ON

TWITTER - @GerryCullen15

THE VATICAN MONSIGNOR

THE SAVIOUR'S COMING

COPYRIGHT - 2024
GERRY CULLEN

MY VERY REAL STORY CONTINUES TODAY

This true-life story includes an account of what happened to Gerry Cullen before and after waking up, having had major open-heart surgery at Leeds General Infirmary in March 2018, and the "gift" received from being in an induced coma.
Gerry explains his new found gift within the book. But where it had come from and why he received it, remains a mystery to this day.

A spiritual awakening with messages received in dreams and other unworldly encounters, makes this story a fascinating read, leaving us wondering about life itself and beyond.

FIVE STAR AMAZON REVIEWS ...

With truly moving frankness the author narrates a life-threatening experience, and how it brought him closer to his spiritual life.

An excellent book showing that there is far more to life then we realise and that there is a continuation of our soul after the death of our body.

A great read and one that really makes you think!!!

This book was of particular interest to me because of my line of work. I love hearing about people's experiences with things that are on a different vibration to us earthly beings. The spiritual awakenings that people go through have been documented and discussed since the beginning of time and each person's story is unique in its own way, there are always some similarities on the surface but I encourage you to look a little deeper - you can start with this book.......

The author begins by telling us a little about himself and his life growing up. He then goes into detail about the 'messages' he has received in dreams, these are set out in a sort of diary entry format. He also speaks of visions.

All of the incidents described seem quite insignificant on their own, but when you put them all together they give a much bigger and clearer picture.

There is a lot I could say about this book but seriously, we would be here all day! It's a great read that is sure to inspire and provoke discussion. It really doesn't matter what walk of life you are from, whether you are religious or a non believer. I feel the story should be taken for what it is and that is one gentleman's extraordinary, unique and beautiful experiences which he has chosen to share with the world.

The book, its content and the author himself are a true gift to the world.

5 stars - Laura - The Bookish Hermit

ABOUT THE AUTHOR

Gerry Cullen

My first book, BETWEEN WORLDS: MY TRUE COMA STORY, is a true adaptation of what happened to me, before and after, having major open heart surgery at Leeds General Infirmary in March 2018.

It is a very real and true account of the "gift" I received after being in an induced coma.

My second book, SKY HIGH! COTE D'AZUR, and my third book ANGEL'S EYES/CHRISTMAS ANGELS are both adapted from my series of stories, written for television.

I had never written books or for television prior to being in a coma.

My very real and true story continues today!

FOLLOW MY STORY ON TWITTER - @GerryCullen15

PRAISE FOR AUTHOR

This book was of particular interest to me because of my line of work. I love hearing about people's experiences with things that are on a different vibration to us earthly beings. The spiritual awakenings that people go through have been documented and discussed since the beginning of time and each person's story is unique in its own way, there are always some similarities on the surface but I encourage you to look a little deeper - you can start with this book…….

The author begins by telling us a little about himself and his life growing up. He then goes into detail about the 'messages' he has received in dreams, these are set out in a sort of diary entry format. He also speaks of visions.

All of the incidents described seem quite insignificant on their own, but when you put them all together they give a much bigger and clearer picture.

There is a lot I could say about this book but seriously, we would be here all day! It's a great read that is sure to inspire and provoke discussion. It really doesn't matter what walk of life you are from, whether you are religious or a non believer. I feel the story should be taken for what it is and that is one gentleman's extraordinary, unique and beautiful experiences which he has chosen to share with the world.

The book, its content and the author himself are a true gift to the world.
*- LAURA - THE BOOKISH HERMIT ***** 5 STARS AMAZON*

- BETWEEN WORLDS: MY TRUE COMA STORY

This book has had one review to date.

It has been given 3 stars by an unknown reader!

- SKY HIGH! COTE D'AZUR

"Angels Eyes" by Gerry Cullen is a heartwarming and enchanting collection of seasonal stories that follows the adventures of Rebecca, Mary, John Paul, and Nicola, who have been reassigned by Michael the Archangel to become proprietors of the CHRISTMAS ANGELS shop in York. As they assume their roles as shopkeepers with a difference, the Angels become involved in a series of angelic and human situations that are filled with the magic of

Christmas.

Set in various locations in York, the stories are imbued with a magical Christmas feeling that is sure to warm the hearts of readers. The characters' true identities as Angels are kept secret throughout the stories, adding an element of mystery and intrigue.

"Angels Eyes" is a delightful and uplifting read that captures the spirit of Christmas and the joy of the holiday season. Gerry Cullen's writing is engaging and filled with charm, making this book a perfect choice for anyone looking for a heartwarming holiday read.

*LAURA - THE BOOKISH HERMIT ***** 5 STARS AMAZON*

- ANGEL'S EYES/CHRISTMAS ANGELS

THE VATICAN MONSIGNOR

A GRIPPING SERIES OF PSYCOLOGICAL THRILLER STORIES SET IN VATICAN CITY AND AROUND THE WORLD.

FOLLOW THE VATICAN MONSIGNOR AS HE INVESTIGATES UNEXPLAINED PHENOMENON TO FIND ANSWERS, WITH HEART POUNDING TWISTS AND TURNS ALONG THE WAY!

The Vatican Monsignor - Book Two

THE NEXT BOOK IN THE SERIES WILL BE IN 2025

BOOKS BY THIS AUTHOR

Between Worlds: My True Coma Story

This true-life story includes an account of what happened to Gerry Cullen before and after waking up, having had major open-heart surgery at Leeds General Infirmary in March 2018, and the "gift" received from being in an induced coma.
Gerry explains his new found gift within the book. But where it had come from and why he received it, remains a mystery to this day.

A spiritual awakening with messages received in dreams and other unworldly encounters, makes this story a fascinating read, leaving us wondering about life itself and beyond.

Sky High! Cote D'azur

Nice, sun kissed jewel of the French Riviera. A popular tourist destination for the rich and famous.

When a British MI6 agent goes missing after being on attachment to the Commissariat de Police in Nice, a Specialist Task Force is set up on the Cote D'Azur to assist the Police in cracking crime on the Continent.

Three "Ghost Operatives" are drafted in by British Intelligence under an alias. Countess Suzanna Minori is placed in charge of unit in liaison with Mark Taylor in London.

In a series of assignments on the Cote D'Azur and in London suave Simon King, rough diamond Steve McBride and new recruit Bethany Williams are the "ghost" agents working under the code name: SKY HIGH!

Amazing picturesque locations on the French Riviera taking in Monte Carlo, Monaco, Cannes and Nice add to the charm, character and atmosphere of the series of stories.

Stylish, chic, gripping with just the right amount of panache!

Action adventure guaranteed!

C'est la vie!

Angel's Eyes/Christmas Angels

ANGEL'S EYES - The Angel private eyes, with a

difference, undertake anything with a twist, they are all real angels!

Angel's: Rebecca, Mary, John Paul and Nicola have been sent by Michael the Archangel to LEEDS, West Yorkshire, and the ancient city of YORK to investigate all types of problems, from all levels of society.

The Angel's are aiming to find, and guide, lost souls, to protect those in distress, and to help those without a cause.

They have been charged to give sight to those who cannot see, whatever the problem, and to heal the sick and incurable.

All the Angel's will have to undertake their assignments while also being human on Earth at the same time!

They do not want to get their wings, they already have them!

While under the protection of Heaven, they will also be able to cloak themselves in disguise!

The Angel's are ready to assist anyone who needs their help in this stylish set of stories.

The Angel's will encounter the Grey Lady, the ghostly Centurion and a cohort of Roman soldiers, Dick Turpin and Guy Fawkes along the way.

The Angel's will also experience Speed Dating and various other problems in a very modern day World!

CHRISTMAS ANGELS - This seasonal set of stories reunites Rebecca, Mary, John Paul and Nicola.

The Angel's have been reassigned by Michael the Archangel and assume the roles of Proprietors of

the famous CHRISTMAS ANGELS shop in YORK, on a short term lease, with a view to being permanent!
However, they are shop keepers with a difference!
The Angel's become engaged in various angelic and human situations, all with a magical Christmas feeling!
The stories take place at various settings in YORK.
Will the Angel's be found out, or will their true identities remain an angelic secret?

Printed in Great Britain
by Amazon